TALES FROM THE TRAIN
EVERYBODY HAS A STORY TO TELL

BY THE SAME AUTHOR

The Devil's Tears
Silent Night

The Singhing Detective Series
The Singhing Detective
The Godfathers of London
Sugar and Spice
A Walk on the Wild Side

TALES FROM THE TRAIN: EVERYBODY HAS A STORY TO TELL

M. C. DUTTON

Copyright © 2025 M C Dutton

The moral right of the author has been asserted.

Apart from any fair dealing for the purposes of research or private study, or criticism or review, as permitted under the Copyright, Designs and Patents Act 1988, this publication may only be reproduced, stored or transmitted, in any form or by any means, with the prior permission in writing of the publishers, or in the case of reprographic reproduction in accordance with the terms of licences issued by the Copyright Licensing Agency. Enquiries concerning reproduction outside those terms should be sent to the publishers. This is a work of fiction. Names, characters, businesses, places, events and incidents are either the products of the author's imagination or used in a fictitious manner. Any resemblance to actual persons, living or dead, or actual events is purely coincidental.

Troubador Publishing Ltd
Unit E2 Airfield Business Park,
Harrison Road, Market Harborough,
Leicestershire LE16 7UL
Tel: 0116 279 2299
Email: books@troubador.co.uk
Web: www.troubador.co.uk

ISBN 978-1-83628-083-5

British Library Cataloguing in Publication Data.
A catalogue record for this book is available from the British Library.

Printed and bound in the UK by TJ Books Limited, Padstow, Cornwall
Typeset in 11.5pt Adobe Garamond Pro by Troubador Publishing Ltd, Leicester, UK

I dedicate this book to my wonderful Sister **Pamela Maria Cumberworth.** She was my best friend, my reader, my critic and she loved my books. I would have nothing printed until she approved. Rest in Peace darling Pam.

Richard Charles Gay, my creative cover designer. Thank you so much.

Family is everything – to my wonderful children **Helen, Richard and Amanda, Andrew and Nansal.** My darling grandchildren **Isabella, Kiera, Rebecca, Josh, Thomas, Bradley, Max, Edie-Rose.** And my darling Great Grandchildren **Thea and Jude.** I am truly blessed.

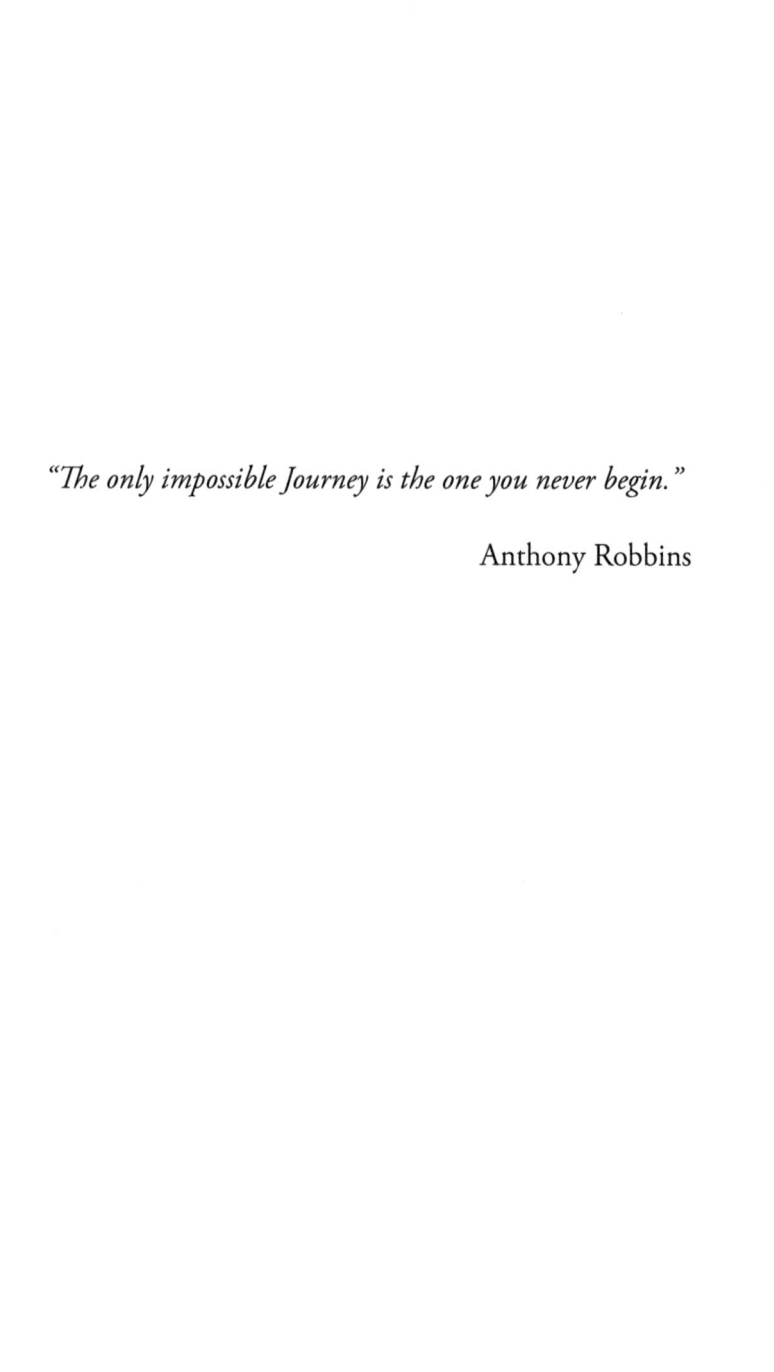

"The only impossible Journey is the one you never begin."

Anthony Robbins

CONTENTS

It's Good to Talk	1
A Sentimental Journey	10
Polite Conversation	14
Fairy Tales	22
Family Life	28
Mother Knows Best	36
The Grass is Greener	42
The Red Beret	50
The Speech	59
The Watch	69
Those Were the Days, My Friend	76
Pot Black	85

IT'S GOOD TO TALK

Sandra Dee Blackstock, she always used her first and second name; believing that Sandra Dee sounded like a film star. The train had been stationery for a while now and she could feel the heat building up. She had put on her best blue flower dress which was in a silk material with the darker blue long-sleeved jacket. She hadn't worn it for ages, and it always made her feel quite regal. Travelling to London was one of those occasions that needed a bit of special attention. The carriage was quite full and she didn't want to draw attention to herself but she had to take the jacket off, she felt very warm and could feel beads of sweat forming on her forehead; she couldn't bear to look a mess, or for heaven's sake smell of BO, the thought made her blush. She quickly took a perfume bottle from her bag and sprayed her neck; she was going to smell of nothing but Estée Lauder Youth Dew. She had worn it for such a long time that she couldn't smell the heavy scent anymore, but from the looks given in her direction, everyone else in the carriage could. *Lucky them*, she thought.

She took off her jacket and folded it very carefully, putting it on the rack above her head. It was lucky she had brought with her a new *Woman's Realm* magazine to read, or she would have been quite bored. She desperately wanted to read the letters again but knew she couldn't in front of all these people because they would make her cry and she couldn't cope with the embarrassment.

Duncan was in London, where he had a contract job to do. He was an excellent electrician who was in great demand. She was very proud of him. They had been married for 15 years. He had always provided for them both. They hadn't been blessed with children but she was still hopeful it would happen one day, at 35 years old she still had time. Duncan was her childhood sweetheart. They had never, and she licked her lips as she tried to find the right words, they had never been an explosive couple. They had never rowed, well, except for the time she had said she didn't want to watch a programme and he did, but it wasn't really much of a row because she went off and washed up the Sunday-dinner plates and he watched his programme. That's about as bad a row as they ever had. There had never been an explosion of passion either, but that was another matter. Instinctively she glanced around the carriage as those thoughts sprang to mind. Well, they met at school and sort of drifted into marriage after a 6-year courtship. They did love each other and Duncan had always been a wonderful provider. He worked very hard and she kept a good home for him to return to. He went away quite a bit; the work as a contract electrician took him all over the country. Still, to keep herself busy she had her job in the Co-op on the tills. She loved the cheery gossip and knew most of the customers. She only worked part-time. Her role was to look after Duncan when he came home. Her life was good, she conceded that perhaps some people would think it a little dull, but she and Duncan liked it that way. He always said to her, "Sandra Dee, you are for me." It was his little joke and they always laughed when he said it.

Duncan was not big on words in the romantic sense. A bit of her would have liked to have been pulled into his arms and told how much he loved her and how he would fight the wildest animal to save her. She smiled to herself at such a silly thought. Her Duncan was not that type of man, he was quiet, and liked to think a lot. If he said anything, you listened because he said very little. He loved her in ways that were just as good. He was never out of work and when he got home, he would do all the little repair jobs that needed doing without complaining. He painted and decorated regularly and gave her enough money to buy nice things for the house. He appreciated all she did for him. He said no one else could cook like she did or iron a shirt so well.

Duncan had been adventurous once she remembered. When they got married, he was determined they would own their own house. Both their parents rented their flats from the council. They thought he was getting above his station and told him he could never afford such a thing. Sandra remembered how scared and proud and breathless she felt with her Duncan standing up to their parents in such a way.

Duncan had left school and got an apprenticeship as an electrician with Boggis and Sons, just around the corner from where they lived. They were good to Duncan and he got all his qualifications and became one of their top electricians. They were married just after he qualified and went to live with Duncan's parents, in the spare room. It was a bit cramped but they knew it wouldn't be for long. They had been on the council waiting list since they got engaged and were hoping to get their own flat. Duncan's mother was in contact with the council on a weekly basis and reckoned they would get a flat in no time at all.

Life had been comfortable, she enjoyed being married and was looking forward to having their own place soon. When Duncan announced he was going to buy a house and not live in a council flat, ripples of derision ran through the families. They worried he was getting above himself. They had conceded that he had passed his exams and was a proper electrician but buying a house, was well, it was like saying he was rich or something or had won the lottery. Everyone knew that wasn't going to happen.

No one ever remembered Duncan standing up to anyone before. He had always been a good lad and listened to his elders but now he would have none of it. Sandra stood by him, even though she was very scared. She had whispered once to her mother that Duncan had said they would have a mortgage payment to make every month and that houses cost thousands of pounds. She wondered if they would ever earn enough to pay for the house. Her mother, perplexed at such an idea, said she was always welcome to come back home if Duncan continued with such ideas. Sandra never talked to her mother about such things again. There was no way she would leave her Duncan.

Duncan told her in the privacy of the spare room that he wanted to buy a house for her and for the children they would have. In that moment she felt she would burst with love and pride. How did she get so lucky to marry such a fine man?

He got a mortgage and they bought a house not far from where they had been brought up. It needed work doing to it but again, Duncan promised he would work hard. They had the house for 2 years and Duncan had kept his promise and they were happy. When the recession hit, Boggis and Son teetered for a while and finally had to close down and Duncan was out of work.

This was the most horrific time for Sandra. A mortgage to pay and no money coming in but the little bit she earned at the Co-op. She said nothing to Duncan but he had seen how worried and scared she was. He promised her that everything would be all right, and it was. He went out every day looking for work. He took any job he could find; even a paper round for a while.

They got through it, even though it took seven months of scrimping and making do. Duncan eventually found a job with a facility company in London that looked after buildings around the country. It was a good company and if there was any work close to where they lived, Duncan always got those jobs. Even so, he had to be away from home for many weeks in the year. It was hard at first but they both got used to it after a while. Duncan worked hard and always provided for them. *Yes*, she thought, *he is a good man*.

She was sitting on this train, which had stopped now for nearly 2 hours, and she was worried she would arrive far too late in London to surprise him at his lodgings. It would be bad manners to arrive at a late hour, his landlady would be cross.

He had been away for their 15th Wedding Anniversary this week. He had sent a card and a note saying they would go out to the Harvester Pub for a meal on his return. They always went there and they liked it. It wasn't too posh or anything and they felt comfortable. He phoned on their anniversary but he never had much to say; he didn't make a habit of ringing, but she knew he was thinking of her. She had her girlfriends to chat to and didn't mind his lack of conversation, although… And she stopped herself again, for being so silly. With a sigh she reminded herself, *Duncan is a good man.*

He had been really good when she went to the doctor to find out why she hadn't fallen pregnant. The doctor said something about fallopian tubes and things like that. Sandra Dee never understood stuff like that and it was too upsetting to listen to. Duncan had told her it didn't matter, that they were all right as they were and a baby would disrupt their life anyway. Sandra Dee had cried a little at the loss of babies, but agreed they were fine as they were and they had each other and that was enough. She knew there were things she could most probably do but she didn't like the idea of all those tests and being in hospital and Duncan hadn't pushed her in that direction, he was very considerate.

So, it was a tremendous shock to her to find the letters. She had been doing some spring cleaning, well it wasn't spring but she always called it spring cleaning, it was her little joke. In going through cupboards and drawers she found a small zip-up bag that belonged to Duncan. She had seen it before and had never touched it. She was always respectful of his property. She hadn't known what got into her but, she just had to open it, she felt bad and deceitful, but open it she did. It served her right. Her mother had always said that bad intentions bring bad problems and she was right. The bag was stuffed with letters. They were not work letters. They were not addressed to anyone in particular but she knew they were love letters.

It would be an hour before she read them. She zipped up the bag again and took it downstairs to the dining table and carefully laid it there. She went off and dusted the bedroom, polished the mirrors, vacuumed the carpet, fiddled with the pillows to make sure they were straight and creases smoothed out. Finally, she could not put it off any more. She went to the kitchen, made a cup of tea and carried it to the dining table. She wished she hadn't opened the bag but once opened she had to read the contents. With a fearful trepidation and feeling as if her predictable, safe life was slipping out of her reach, Sandra Dee took hold of the first letter.

With a deep breath and tears so close, she rummaged in her apron for a tissue and she read the date on the first letter. He had written it only days before he left for the present job. She read how he loved and worshipped this woman like no other. She read words so painfully poignant about her beauty of soul and looks, words she didn't think he even knew. He loved another woman. She sat for hours with her tea getting cold, just held in a place she called hell, unable to think or move or cry. The shock felt terminal, the sadness corrosive, the loss was suicidal.

It was dark by the time she thought to read another letter. By now she was set in a cold and fortified manner that would not allow grief to enter. The second letter was dated a year ago, and the third letter the year before that. They all expressed a love that had never been expressed to her. He said things she dreamed of. All these years and he loved someone else? How could he? How could he do this to her and be so deceitful and treacherous. She wanted to rip them all up, to spit in his face and throw the papers at him and call him a rotten, dirty bastard! She was shaking with a venomous hatred that scared her. She would make him pay! She would go to London and confront him. She went into the Co-op the next day and booked two days off work; however impulsive she felt, she wouldn't let work down.

So here she was sitting on a train on the way to London to surprise him. He would have finished work by the time she arrived. He would most probably have showered and changed and be sitting down to his supper in the guest house. She would make her entrance and watch his shocked face at seeing her standing there. She smiled at the thought.

Sitting on the train, just waiting for the journey to start again, she really wanted to read the letters again but she couldn't, she was too emotional and everyone around her would see her tears. She thought back to the day she read them. The last letter was hidden in an inner zipped pouch and when she read it, she knew who the other woman was.

Just thinking of the words in that letter made her eyes prick with tears. It was so tender and caring and so very sad and beautiful and full of longing. He had written about the lost babies and told her how much he loved her and how he had cried for the babies that would not be born. He cried for her knowing she would never know motherhood. He said he wanted to kiss every tear she shed. He loved her more than his life and all the babies' lives; without her he was nothing and he would die rather than lose her. He wrote, "Sandra Dee, you are for me," for always and ever.

She was the other woman.

She would make him pay for those letters… for keeping them secret. Oh yes, she was going to show him what a real woman was like by loving him and hugging him and being all the things he had written about.

She couldn't wait to reach London to see the man of her dreams, the man she always wanted. He was her knight and she would honour him.

A SENTIMENTAL JOURNEY

They were going to be late for their connecting trains. "It's always a worry on this line," she said with furrowed brow. He agreed and gently shook her arm to reassure her. This train had been at a standstill now for over an hour and everyone was restless. With nothing to do, a few passengers watched this couple gently interacting and lovingly holding hands. They noticed the wedding rings. One thought ruefully that you don't see many happy married couples these days. This couple looked very happy indeed. They even had reassuring cuddles and a little peck on the cheek too. One passenger thought that a bit much and wanted to say *get a room* but they knew it was just jealousy. You don't often see a married couple talking to each other, let alone hugging each other.

Another passenger reckoned they must be in their late 30s or early 40s. They were going to be late home tonight. It was a Friday and there were many businesses in Portsmouth and it was usual for a good percentage of people to work all week there and then go home to various areas and London was the connection to home for the weekend. It was surmised that it was really lovely to see a married couple working together and travelling together.

She was called Stephanie and he was Richard. They had been together for the past 10 years. They met when working in Portsmouth; he was a premises manager for a freight company and Stephanie was his secretary. It had been lust at first sight as Richard had put it. Stephanie still laughed at this comment. The attraction was physical and within days of working together they were in bed together. This developed into a deep and meaningful love of each other. Neither had ever experienced such unity. They had magnificent sex with a motivational mindset that meant they were perfect for each other. She was highly intelligent and he loved that in her and their conversations were long and satisfying. Their partnership was awesome and at work no one could fault anything they did.

They rented a small flat in Portsmouth. It was only for weekdays when working there because they left for their more substantial home for long weekends. They worked from Tuesday to Friday and the days were long but they had Saturday to Monday off. They called their flat in Portsmouth their love nest, it always made them laugh but it also made them very flirtatious and horny. The days might be long but the nights were longer. They would often say that they needed the rest when they got home because their love life would take a rest too.

This train had a history of hold-ups and both Stephanie and Richard were aware of this. They were booked on the next train from London to home and they always made sure it was at least an hour later than the arrival time from Portsmouth but today this train delay was longer.

"Don't worry, darling, if push comes to shove, we can book into a hotel. If this goes on much longer, I will google an hotel and get us booked in."

She nodded with a smile. He was always so thorough and considerate. She loved him so much. It was a worry though. She knew she had to be at home tomorrow because there was a luncheon to attend. It had been organised many months ago and there would be anger if she didn't attend. The luncheon was to celebrate her parents' 50th wedding anniversary and all the family would be there. Her family did not approve of her working away in Portsmouth all week and there had been many difficult conversations and some anger that she left her parents, who were aged and not well, to be looked after and cared for by other family members.

Richard, well aware of the worry about family and the luncheon, tried to reassure her.

"Don't worry, if we stay over tonight, there will be an early morning train that will get you home well in time for the luncheon. I will make sure you are up."

She smiled, he was so thoughtful and he always made her feel safe and looked after. It was at that point that the overhead speaker crackled and a disembodied voice informed everyone on board that the train was about to start. It said that the driver would do his best to make up some of the time and connecting trains in London might not be compromised.

With relief, everyone visibly relaxed as the train started and moved faster than usual. Stephanie and Richard looked at each other ruefully.

"I know," said Stephanie. "It's good if we catch the connecting trains we are booked on but," and she smiled cheekily, "I quite liked the idea of a night in a hotel with you." They both laughed and held hands. Richard gave a reassuring squeeze. The lady near them felt quite emotional looking at this very loving couple.

They arrived at the station with minutes to spare for connecting trains. Stephanie and Richard grabbed their bags and rushed off the train in the hope they would be in time. A guard said the connecting trains would be leaving 10 minutes late so they had enough time to get to the platform and on board.

They had enough time to say goodbye. They said goodbye every week so it was nothing special, it was normal. Why it felt different today, they didn't know. The parting was painful and reluctantly Stephanie was to catch her train into Essex and Richard was to catch his train to Suffolk.

Their respective partners would be waiting with a hot supper and a glass of something nice to welcome them home for the weekend. Stephanie's husband, a civil servant who commuted to London every day, and as he would tell her, waited for the weekends to arrive so he could be with Stephanie. Richard's wife, a housewife and a member of the local Women's Institute, would happily regale all the gossip to him that had accrued over the week and he would listen intently.

Stephanie and Richard longed for the weekends to be over so they could be together. *See you on Tuesday morning to catch the 7.45a.m. train to Portsmouth,* was whispered when they would be a couple again.

POLITE CONVERSATION

He fidgeted in his seat. He felt prickly and tried hard to keep his impatience hidden. He looked across at her, she was still talking. He wondered why women had to make huge conversations out of things that only require a sentence. Mrs Vera Wentworth-Smythe was her name. She had shared this information with him as she extended a beautifully gloved hand for him to shake, although for a moment he wasn't sure if she meant for him to kiss it. It was his job to listen, and even if he was trapped on a damned train that had stopped for a hellish two hours so far, he was finding it hard to concentrate. He wouldn't get back home until bloody midnight even if it moved now and he had to be in the office at eight in the morning. He felt himself flush with anxiety.

"So, Police Inspector, what do you think of that?" she asked in her beautifully modulated voice, her head tilted to one side as she looked into his eyes. He thought the hat might have encouraged the tilt but it was a very classy pose. He thought she looked a bit like Miss Marple, the one on television. That same small frame and genteel manner that showed she came from a different era. She was far more sophisticated and gracious than any woman he had ever met. Her money was not spent on plastic surgery, that was for sure. She was a 70-year-old woman who looked her age. He mused that any woman who could afford to sit in First Class and who was dressed in that peculiarly plain but expensive style certainly had a style and quiet understated manner that showed she was nothing if not top-drawer. She gave him an understanding smile as she repeated her question.

She noted he was distracted. He was obviously in his 50s, but had his hair cut in what she understood to be known quaintly as a number one cut. It was white so he looked almost bald. She preferred men who wore hats. She sighed in disappointment. Not many men did these days. He had been good-looking in his prime, she ventured, but had been ravaged by time. His lean, tall body and the heavily etched lines around his mouth and eyes gave him an intense and stern look. She could see he was not a happy man.

"Would you like a cup of tea, dear?" she repeated in that soft and caring way she had learned to cultivate. "You must be so fed up with the wait."

She was right there; he could do with stretching his legs and he decided he would get them both a cup of tea and a biscuit.

When he returned, he felt better for the short walk and settled to enjoy his tea. She did her best to grasp the plastic cup; he noted she was obviously not used to such things. He had got the man in the buffet car to find a plastic cup holder for her, and she smiled with gratitude at his consideration. They sat in silence for the first few sips and he watched her with interest and noted she would look into the distance for a few seconds and then with an intake of breath regale him with a story about her dear departed husband and the wonderful times they had sailing his yacht, the glamorous life they had and the wonderful balls.

He saw her eyes mist up at the memories. She told him how she had curtsied to the Queen and how Prince Philip had crushed her hand when he shook it. She talked about their home in Knightsbridge, who they entertained and the country home in Gloucester and the weekend parties. As she spoke, she mopped the corners of her mouth with a small lace handkerchief. He was fascinated by the action, nothing escaped from her, not even the tiniest dribble.

He knew he wasn't meant to do it, but he had had enough of "so and so doing this", and "Harrods sent that". It was time to be belligerent.

"So, Mrs Wentworth-Smythe, why did you kill them?"

She looked at him in disgusted horror, almost as if he had asked what size knickers she wore. "I think that is a most vulgar question, Inspector. I don't expect you to have quite the manners of my generation or standing, but I had hoped you would phrase your questions and comments in more acceptable language."

He was quite nonplussed. She was accusing him of bad manners and her tone had brought him close to apologising. He told himself to get a grip. He knew he wasn't very good with women. Having never married, the art of talking easily to women had passed him by. All he knew was they cried if you were too tough and that got you nowhere in an investigation. He was known in the force for being focussed.

They had met 20 years ago when he was investigating the disappearance of Mr Wentworth-Smythe and a Miss Jane Stowell. He had never given up on the case. The bodies had never been found and the verdict was left open. The file had never closed but gathered dust on a shelf and had been reviewed by him regularly over the years. He was known as the Mountie at the Yard. The joke was he always got his man but no woman would have him. But today was to be the pinnacle of a long, painstaking investigation. He was taking her back to Scotland Yard and she would be charged with murder. He finally had the evidence to implicate her.

He asked again: "Were you responsible for the disappearance of Mr Wentworth-Smythe and Miss Jane Stowell?"

She looked into the distance for a moment and her brow knotted while she gathered her thoughts.

"Well, dear, I suppose I was," she reflected.

He stayed quiet and waited. It was as if she was about to regale him with one of her little stories.

"Was it jealousy?" he asked. She looked at him again, with horror.

"Oh dear, what a silly thing to say. Of course not. I loved him and jealousy is such a vulgar emotion, don't you think?"

He nodded and asked if she would tell him what happened in her own words. With an inclination of her head, she smiled and leaned forward and tapped him on the knee and said she would tell him everything because she couldn't have him misunderstanding.

"It was quite simple really. I had no choice. Miss Stowell was his mistress and she had been invited along for the cruise around the Isle of Wight. My husband was particularly fond of the Isle of Wight and in his younger days he would race during Cowes."

"How did you feel about Mr Wentworth-Smythe bringing his mistress on the cruise with you on board as well?" Inspector Alan Cray asked.

She looked at him and smiled.

"My dear, I was grateful to her. I didn't want to bother myself with such things. She kept him amused and I found that very suitable."

He frowned. Why had she murdered them both? *Murder is not a lazy emotion*, he thought. It takes fire and she didn't look like she had any fire to stoke. He was now fascinated and leaned forward to hear her every word.

She picked a piece of imaginary fluff off her shoulder, brushed her sleeve absent-mindedly and looking straight into his eyes with a quiet defiance – "My dear, it is quite simple, really. Mistresses are an acceptable necessity in most marriages, I find, but they have to be kept in their place. My husband started to put her first. The staff noticed. I was becoming second place and that couldn't happen. The final straw was at dinner. He sat her next to him and that was a blatant snub. Mr Wentworth-Smythe had many qualities, my dear, but he just wasn't sensible in his dealings with Miss Stowell. We would have been the talk of the town and a laughing stock to boot. Our friends and our standing in society would suffer and I am afraid that couldn't happen. So, I planned to let them go."

He found her calm, almost endearing confession unbelievable. Over the years he had heard some pretty rum excuses for murder but sitting in the wrong seat at dinner took the biscuit.

What was left of the bodies had been found in a large cask at the bottom of the sea off Cowes by a local diving club. They were identified by rings that had fallen off Miss Stowell's fingers and by his denture plates. The inspector had got a telephone call that took him from London to the Isle of Wight where Mrs Wentworth-Smythe had a house.

"You must have had help. You couldn't have done it alone," he ventured.

She smiled again and after a brief moment continued. "Of course I had help. My butler John helped me. He is *such* a good and loyal servant. He is still with me after all these years; he will never leave me even though he is now 75."

The inspector made a mental note to arrest John as soon as they arrived back in London.

"It wasn't an unpleasant demise for them, Inspector. I poisoned them. John got the potion for me and I put it in their drinks. I feel they died happy and contented with each other. We sat on the deck for the last evening; I encouraged that because it would be easy for John to dispose of them."

She looked a little whimsical and the inspector wondered what was going through her mind. She had implicated John and that surprised him.

"I left the deck when they seemed to have faded away and left John to put them in the trunk and push them overboard. John said it was deep water and the trunk would stay hidden. For all anybody was aware, they had got very drunk and fallen overboard when no one was around. Everyone on board knew I had gone to bed earlier."

The silence was long... she stared into Alan Cray's eyes smiling kindly.

"Are you alright, Inspector? You seem a little under the weather," she asked with concern. "Can I get you a drink of water?"

He shook his head. He had to think. He had a full and frank confession and she had implicated the butler as well. Why didn't he turn on his tape recorder? Why the hell didn't he bring it with him? Damn! He was shaking and feeling quite giddy with the excitement of it all. He had his mobile somewhere. With shaking hands he tried to find it but it was nowhere on him. He went to stand up and look on the rack above to see if it was there, but he felt dizzy.

"What about a drink, Inspector, would you like one?" she was asking him.

He nodded this time and took a glass of water that had been handed to him. She mopped his brow with her handkerchief and said soothing words to help him calm down. He loosened his collar and asked if the window might be opened. He felt a little better as the air rushed in and cooled him.

He sat quietly for a moment and then turned slightly and realised the man from the buffet car was there. Mrs Wentworth-Smythe had turned and said, "Thank you, John," as the window was opened.

Strange that she would know the buffet man's name... but he felt so tired and closed his eyes.

There was a jerking movement and the train started. She told him that they were on their way now and would be home soon. Her voice was trailing away. She was saying goodbye and how lovely it had been to meet him….

FAIRY TALES

She shook the paper violently open and then felt rather embarrassed. She looked up to see if the harassed mother opposite her noticed. In the close proximity of a train carriage she realised it was not good to show her temper in public. Clarissa Kemp was well known in the modelling world for temper tantrums and diva ways. Today she wanted anonymity and calm, but what she had was a fucking train standing still in the middle of nowhere for 2 hours and extreme tension! Tension, as her makeup woman says, is so bad for the lines on the face, she had to calm down. She needed to be in London and have a restful sleep in her hotel tonight to prepare her for tomorrow. It wasn't just the baby crying that got on her nerves, it was the kid wandering up and down the small space; she wanted to scream, "Sit down, brat, and shut up!" But of course she couldn't.

It wasn't often she felt uneasy. Clarissa was quite successful and at 22 years old had a few more years before the bubble would burst. Men adored her and wanted her but Gerry loved her and she appreciated his devotion and that is why she married him last year. Coming to London was so treacherous. She hated lying to him, telling him she was seeing a girlfriend and going on a shopping spree; he would never understand the real reason.

She looked up from her paper to see the kid standing there just staring at her silently. Her big blue eyes unblinking, she didn't move. The kid was ugly, no hair and was fat, Clarissa hated anything fat! Her red cardigan was too tight for her. *Don't mothers know how to dress their kids?* she thought in disgust. Clarissa would not be seen anywhere without everything matching, her long, sleek auburn hair perfectly straight and fussed over every day by Deano, makeup immaculate and nails, she was well known for her nails; long and perfectly shaped. At six-foot-tall Clarissa had always looked down on people, humility never got in the way of the clear view that she was a super star and everyone wanted to be like her.

After a minute of Clarissa holding the stare of this kid, the mother broke the silence and leaned forward and confided in a whisper, "She thinks you're the Fairy Queen."

Clarissa smiled and nodded, and wondered what that meant. The mother, in the same whisper, introduced herself as Tracy from Southampton, and Clarissa nodded and said her name and with a smile went back to her paper. Tracy leaned forward and in a loud and upbeat voice spoke to the kid.

"Molly, sweetheart, this is Clarissa, say hello."

Clarissa was forced to look at the ugly kid again and wait for the hello which never came.

The confidential whisper returned with Tracy saying, "She is shy, Clarissa, sorry, but she has a big day tomorrow and she has had so much to put up with lately that I think she has forgotten her manners." The loud upbeat voice returned as the mother spoke to the kid.

"Sweetheart, Clarissa isn't a Fairy Queen, she is a lady on the train."

Molly didn't say a word and her eyes never left Clarissa, still staring she shook her head.

Clarissa looked at the mother and gave her a quizzical look and was just about to ask what the heck was going on here when Tracy again leant forward and again in a whisper told Clarissa about the operations Molly had had in her short 4 years and how the cancer had gone into remission after chemotherapy and that was why she had no hair. She was on steroids which made her a little chunky. Again, the loud upbeat voice appeared and Tracy joyfully said, "Molly, we are seeing the nice doctor tomorrow, aren't we? Don't they love you in the hospital and we have to visit all the nurses don't we?"

Molly, still eyes locked on Clarissa, nodded and smiled.

Back to the whisper, Tracy almost mouthed the words and Clarissa had to lean further forward to catch what was being said.

"It's looking a little difficult tomorrow. They think there is something on the scan we need to talk about and it's all a little worrying, but we have fought lots of battles, and won."

Clarissa felt a tear whelming up, she wasn't ready to hear this. But the loud upbeat voice appeared again.

"Hey, Molly, tell Clarissa about the holiday we are saving for." She gave the little girl a playful rub on the back. Molly smiled. Still looking at Clarissa, she blinked and told her in a strong voice about Disneyland in

America and how she was going to have her photo taken and she was going on the rides and how she wanted to meet Donald Duck. Clarissa saw her face light up and you know what? The child was beautiful, she had a smile that warmed Clarissa.

The baby on Tracy's lap had been sleeping but woke with a start, all that leaning forward had disturbed him. Tracy looked thin and gaunt but managed to produce a pretty large boob and proceeded to feed the baby. Clarissa thought, *Where was the husband in all of this, typical! They go and have fun and leave the women to do all the dirty work.*

Clarissa asked Molly when she was going to Disneyland. She thought sullenly that it was a sure bet the father would go on that trip. She was feeling sorry for the mother and Molly was still staring. She was used to people staring at her, it was her job after all, but it was quite disconcerting to have a child stare at you for so long.

"So when is the trip to Disneyland, Tracy?"

She asked to try and break the concentration of Molly's stare. Tracey smiled a jolly smile and with shrug of her shoulders and a throw away lightness of speech she said, "Oh we will see, maybe in a while."

Clarissa thought that Gerry would be great in this situation. He absolutely loved children, in fact when they married, he had said he wanted a large family. Clarissa had smiled and said it would happen, but later. She had no intention of being a mother for a very long time, if ever. So the trip to the hospital tomorrow had to be a secret, Gerry would never understand how important her career was and that a baby would finish it now. She had lots more work to do and all the acting and singing lessons she was taking to further her career would be wasted and lost. A baby was for other people, not her. She had drawn out over a week the two thousand pounds she would need for the hospital; they were exclusive, discreet and very expensive. She didn't want him to check their account and see anything with the hospital name on it. She held her bag close to her, two thousand pounds is still a lot of money to carry around. That is why she was happy to sit in a carriage with just another woman, much safer.

Molly shifted her stance and blinked, she wanted to talk to Clarissa. She asked if she was the Fairy Queen because the Fairy Queen was the beautiful lady who would make her well and make it so her mummy and brother and her lived happily ever after. Tracy, holding the baby tight whilst he was feeding, leaned forward. In that confiding whisper she told Clarissa about the bedtime story that kept Molly going through some of the dark hours. She told her the Fairy Queen was her hope, and her magic wand would be waved and they would all live happily ever after because the Fairy Queen loved Molly and had wonderful powers to make good and happy things happen so everything would be alright. Clarissa found out where the husband was, Tracy told her he was in the Army in Iraq and he was killed just before the baby was born. She said with a watery smile that she missed him dreadfully.

Clarissa, her eyes bulging with contained tears, looked into Molly's eyes and knew what she had to do.

"Yes, Molly, I am the Fairy Queen and everything would be alright, I promise."

She had to tell the kid something good didn't she? The unexpected hug from Molly caught her by surprise and

Clarissa felt a tear escape down her cheek. She brushed it away quickly. She didn't do tears.

The train had moved whilst they were talking and in no time at all they arrived in London.

Clarissa gathered everything together, ready to depart. Molly had stayed close to her for the remainder of the journey and had fallen asleep against her. Clarissa had sat awkwardly stroking Molly's head, feeling the smoothness and softness, not understanding how life could be so cruel.

She said goodbye to Tracy and wished her well and muttered all the empty promises of keeping in touch. As she left the train and hurried along the platform holding her mobile to her ear she said urgently, "Gerry, I am coming back now, I'll explain later." She hesitated for a moment and quietly added, "I love you."

Tracy had put the baby in the pushchair ready to get off the train and went to pick up Molly to put her in the twin buggy. She felt something thick and firm in Molly's waistband and when she pulled it out it was an envelope with a blessed and wonderful two thousand pounds in it. With shaking hands she read the scrawled note which just said Disneyland.

Molly climbed onto the seat where her mother had sat down in shock. With innocent understanding, Molly smiled and brushed the tears from her mother's eyes.

"See, Mummy, everything is going to be alright. I told you she was the beautiful Fairy Queen."

FAMILY LIFE

Michelle rummaged through the two plastic bags she had near her on the train. She checked the presents she had bought were wrapped properly. Nothing worse, she surmised, than a present half open, it spoiled the surprise. She was going home to see her boys.

This happened every week and they had got used to her coming in the door and giving them a present to open. She always wrapped their presents in colourful paper. She had all week to find what she wanted and get it wrapped. She was so excited at the thought of seeing them and cuddling them. Her boys were her life.

Life was not fair and, in some ways, rather cruel. Michelle and Peter, when they got married, had lived in a flat in the Barbican. It was a plush, modern yuppy flat in the heart of London and they enjoyed living there. It was close to work and they had a great life.

Michelle was a premises manager and Peter was a graphic designer. They could have lived a fairy-tale life just doing what they did every day. Money was not a problem and they tasted the expensive side of life with holidays abroad, meals at expensive restaurants and designer clothes. But that wasn't enough for them. They wanted something else. They wanted to be parents and to love and be loved as a family.

It was after 5 years of being together that they decided they wanted to be a family. A flat in London was not suitable they decided. They wanted to live in the country in a big sprawling house that would lend itself to healthy clean living and an environment that was wholesome for their children. They scoured the country for the right place to live. They settled on Hertfordshire. Peter could work from home as long as he wasn't too far from London if he needed to go there. They were adamant that if they had a family then no way would their children be left alone.

Michelle had always thought it would be her that would stay at home with their children; it seemed logical. Unfortunately, Michelle earned far more than Peter and her job was a salaried job. Peter's work was not so regular. Sometimes he worked flat out and he earned a fortune, other times there was nothing coming in. Reluctantly they had decided that they needed a salary that was consistent. They wanted to have a safe and secure life for their children.

When it was time, to their surprise they had two babies. Willie and Freddie were a handful but they loved them like no one has loved a baby before. Michelle's love for her boys shocked her at first. She had never felt such a strong loving emotion. The year off work was the happiest year she had ever experienced. She watched as her boys grew. She played with them and cuddled and kissed them.

Going back to work was devastating. More so, because she had given up her London job to nurse her babies for a year. She knew she wouldn't have any trouble getting another job. Michelle had a fine reputation in the corporate world and was regularly headhunted. But something had happened during the year she was off work. The recession had caused a lot of redundancies and all the companies she thought would beg her to work for them had fallen silent.

It was a worrying time. They needed the money to maintain their lifestyle and they needed to care for their babies. Eventually a job was offered to Michelle but it would mean she had to stay away from home for the week. It was an American company in Portsmouth. They were offering a very good salary and accommodation for the week.

After much tears Michelle reluctantly accepted the job. Peter promised earnestly that when she came home at the weekends she would have nothing to do except be with her babies. Willie and Freddie were hers for the weekend. He unrealistically said that the hours she spent with them at the weekend would be the same if not more than the time she would have with them if she came home every night. She tried to cling on to that thought.

It was so hard. To be parted from her babies tore Michelle's heart to pieces. She talked to them on the phone every day but it wasn't the same. Peter was really good and he did all the housework and cooked for them. She hadn't cooked or cleaned for years now.

They lived near a forest and close to the River Lea. She would spend the weekend playing with the boys and they would walk in the forest and by the river. They slept in her bed too. No way would she be parted from them for the weekend. Peter never seemed to mind. She had bought them new winter coats she had seen in a local shop in Portsmouth. She worried they would catch a cold in the winter when they went for a walk.

When Freddie had a bad cough she left work immediately and went home. No way would she be parted from her baby if he wasn't well. She sighed again. It was so hard being away from them. She did wonder if their idea of living in the country was a good idea. She had tentatively suggested that they all come and live in Portsmouth then she could see her babies every day but Peter said that wasn't practical and begrudgingly she knew he was right.

She was lonely in Portsmouth. Being a premises manager meant she didn't make friends easily. All the people who worked for her were pleasant to her but actually they left to go home or to the pub together. No one had ever asked her to join them. She conceded she ran a tight ship and perhaps she wasn't the kindest of bosses but she knew that she was fair. "Firm but fair" was her saying.

She had pictures of her babies all over her desk. All the different poses that made them so beautiful and cute. She polished the frames every day as she looked at them. No one said much to her about her babies. She wanted to talk about them and tell everyone what they were like and the funny cute things they did, but no one asked. Once, a girl did ask and it was amazing really, but time flew and she realised she had talked about her babies for over an hour. She laughed, embarrassed at having spent so much time talking about her personal life. No one else asked her about her babies.

Now here she was sitting on this train which had

stopped for 2 hours. She was beside herself. She had so little time at home and this would make her late. When she arrived in London, she had to change trains to take her out to Hertfordshire and if she missed the last train… Her thoughts trailed, unable to consider such a dreadful thing. She got her mobile out again; she had rung home twice already. Peter was anxious that she would be very late. She cried quietly into the phone and wished she was home now. She kept her head down, not wanting anyone to see how upset she was.

He put Freddie and Willie on the phone so she could talk to them. She laughed through her tears hearing their excitement at hearing her voice. It calmed her down talking to them. She so wanted to hug them and kiss them. Peter was very kind. He soothingly told her she wouldn't be long now and they would all be waiting for her.

She was so jealous of Peter. He had all day, every day he could spend with Freddie and Willie. She told herself that he had no idea how dreadful this was for her. She was tormented by the fact that Freddie and Willie might love him more than her. There was many a night in her bedsit in Portsmouth that she thought about Peter and the boys. She often asked herself why was it her that had to make all the sacrifices. Why didn't he get a proper job then she could stay at home with the boys. It had been a long time since she and Peter had slept together. The boys took up a lot of room in her bed and besides, it wouldn't be proper if Peter slept in with them as well.

There had been a couple of nights when she had rung home and there was no answer. She did wonder what Peter got up to during the week. Personally, she didn't care a stuff as long as the boys were alright. She couldn't allow the thought that the boys might have someone else making a fuss of them. That would be too much to cope with.

Sitting here on this train going nowhere was suddenly very depressing. She didn't want to think about such things. She tried to gain some solace from knowing that everything she did was for her boys. That they were happy and well-adjusted and healthy was her reward. She hoped they knew how much she loved them.

Again, she opened the carrier bags to check the presents she had bought. She pressed the Sellotape to make sure they were stuck down. She put bows on the presents and the trailing strands of silk tape she had lovingly curled. She smiled to herself as she remembered how excited they got when she walked through the door. They would rush up to her, each wanting to be hugged first. She had two arms and she held them both. They were children and so what they wanted more than a cuddle was the hidden presents they knew she had brought with her. It would make her laugh as they tried to get into the carrier bags containing their surprise.

She didn't know why she made each present look so pretty because they just ripped open each present and in their excitement threw away the paper. Peter and her would laugh as they watched. Peter always had a black bin liner handy to clear up the mess. He would have a hot supper ready for her. The boys sat close to her whilst she ate and she would talk and eat and laugh. It was her happiest of times. Peter just stood back and let her get on with it.

Sitting here now she realised there were very few

people she actually spoke to. An adult conversation other than work didn't seem to happen. Her weekends were taken up with the boys and Peter just got on with what he was doing. She hadn't realised before that actually they never went out anymore and they didn't sit, holding hands, watching a programme on the television like they used to. Until this moment she had never realised that she was lonely.

The train shuddered and started slowly to move. There was a muted cheer in the carriage as everyone sat up straight and knew they were going to get home at last. Michelle looked around and smiled at the couple opposite her. Although they had never spoken, they had experienced this trauma together.

The man ventured that they would be late arriving; Michelle nodded. She reciprocated saying that her children were waiting up for her and she hoped she got home before midnight. The woman opposite added that surely the children would be asleep by the time she got home. Michelle, with pride stated that her boys would always be awake when she got home. She told them they would be too excited to sleep. She added that Mummy coming home was the highlight of their week. The couple opposite nodded and smiled in acknowledgement. The woman said that children were wonderful. Michelle smiled and nodded. She thought they were a nice couple.

They asked if she had a picture of her boys. She said of course she did. She said that Freddie and Willie were the most photographed children in the whole wide world. The couple noticed how animated and excited she had become talking about her boys. They smiled; it was so lovely to see such a proud mother.

Michelle opened her bag and rummaged for her small photo album she carried. She apologised that the pictures were actually a couple of months old and the boys had changed. She added excitedly that children change so quickly as they grow. The couple again smiled with understanding. Michelle found her favourite picture of the boys. They were sitting smiling straight into the camera. She would show them this picture first. As she handed it over to the couple opposite, she added "Don't you think they look like they are saying, *I love you, Mummy.*"

The couple looked at the picture of the two beautiful dogs; border collies, they ventured, sitting upright in the picture. They raised their eyebrows and nodded hesitantly towards a glowing and proud Michelle.

MOTHER KNOWS BEST

She sat quietly. Those around her continually fidgeted, tutted and looked at their watches. The carriage contained six stressed and tired passengers, it had been 2 hours since the train stopped in the middle of nowhere and Jane Beech sat in the corner, an oasis of tranquillity, eyes closed, but they knew she was not asleep by the odd twitch of her mouth.

She had been stared at by her fellow travellers for the past two hours, and with nothing else to look at, each in the carriage had closely scrutinised her and tried to work out who she was and why she might be sitting alone on this journey. She had her eyes closed and was not aware of all the attention she was getting. They rightly surmised she was quite young; at 20 years old, Jane kept the appearance of a younger girl with an Alice band holding back her long mousy hair. She wore a cardigan over a heavy blue cotton pinafore dress, rather dull was the view of the man sitting opposite her. The woman at the end of the carriage thought white ankle socks and flat blue shoes were rather silly for someone her age. They all in their own way agreed she look serene and calm which in the present situation was close to sainthood.

Jane used the time to relax and enjoy the peace and solitude that closed eyes afforded her. In her young life she had never known this kind of peace. From as young as 5 years old, she remembered her mother scolding her, telling her she was a difficult child, and a plain and ungrateful child. Mother had told her as she started infant school that the other children would bully her because she wore thick glasses and was different from the others, and Mother was right. Her life at school was hell. She learned over the years to keep quiet and her head down. They laughed at her clothes, they laughed at her glasses and they laughed when she cried. They taunted her stuttering and called her plain J-J-J Jane. Mother had said that she had to get used to it because that was to be her life, only someone like Mother could ever love her. Mother was right. When she got to senior school, the taunts felt far worse, they ganged up on her and it all became too much to cope with. One morning she couldn't get out of bed, she felt paralysed. The stress was diagnosed and her mother said she couldn't go to school anymore because she was sick. Jane was so grateful and relieved; she found she could move again but the stuttering had got worse. Mother arranged for home lessons and told her every day how lucky she was to have a mother who put up with such a wilful and difficult child. She knew that no other mother would do this. Mother loudly proclaimed on many occasions to Jane that children like her would be sent to an orphanage where no one would love them and no one would care. Jane was told that if she was good, Mother would keep her safe. The terror of being sent to an orphanage stayed with Jane until she was 16 years old and was then taken over by the terror of being thrown into the streets. Mother said that children who were simple in the head and plain like her would never be allowed to stay in a family home. Jane was very lucky and she thanked her mother often for her kindness.

Her stutter was so bad that Jane could not speak quickly enough and her mother spoke for her. Mother was right, people didn't want to spend time waiting to hear her say a word, they were far too busy and Jane never spoke in public, she appeared mute. Mother told everyone that she was simple in the head and this would encourage understanding smiles. It had been a long time since Jane had spoken to another person other than her mother.

On a rare visit to the doctors when Mother explained Jane had a chesty cough and needed some antibiotics, Doctor Manse, a locum, found Jane very interesting and asked why she did not speak. Jane had just shaken her head as was usual. Mother spoke up quickly and said the child was simple and couldn't speak properly.

Jane remembered how it had taken a year for Mother to agree to speech lessons for her, but she did reluctantly agree after much persuasion. The pleasure she got from the lessons could be seen by Dr Manse. To have someone spend time teaching her in this way was wonderful. She took the opportunity to read different books, and Dr Manse, Phillip, she blushed at calling him by his first name, was very kind and told her about contact lenses so she didn't have to wear the thick glasses. He found she was an intelligent girl and had no mental issues. She just had an over-protective mother.

Over the year she blossomed, he took her out and

she learned how to order in a restaurant, how to buy something in a shop, and how to buy a ticket for trains. She had never been very far from her home and only then with her mother.

Her speech improved and she still stuttered but was quite clear and learned how to control the stutter. She would rush home and chatter incessantly to her mother. Her mother said all the chatter would be the death of her. She noted mother was cross with her but didn't know why. Mother told her no good would come of it all.

Mother was right, Dr Phillip Manse was moved without notice to another clinic in London far away from her. Mother had reported him as being obsessive over Jane.

Jane remembered how she had argued and raged at her mother for doing such a cruel thing, that Dr Manse was her friend. Mother told her she was an ungrateful, wilful child and didn't deserve her love because she knew that Jane would leave her just as Jane's father had left her years ago. Jane knew he was a wicked, wilful, ungrateful man and she was just like him, Mother had told her this often. Jane complied with her mother's wishes, the thought of being thrown out of the house onto the streets to fend for herself still filled her with terror.

It was only a week ago that Dr Phillip Manse came to see her. Mother had gone to the shops and Phillip had waited in his car until she had got on the bus. Jane was no longer allowed out, Mother bought everything for her and she stayed indoors and waited for her mother to return. Mother had said she was not to be trusted to do as she was told and if people saw her, they would take her away and put her in a home where no one would love her. He knocked on the door and Jane, frightened by the knock, peered through the window and saw Dr Manse. She rushed to the door excitedly. He said he had come to rescue her, to take her to London to a place where they would help her.

Mother had said he would try and get to her and she was right.

Jane said no to his offer to go away with him now. She couldn't leave her mother and she asked him to go away. He gave her a card with a telephone number and an address in London. He told her that if she ever changed her mind, she could contact him there.

Mother was right, she was simple, and she couldn't ever leave her mother. Who would feed her and clothe her. Mother had said that London was a very bad place full of people who would hurt her and laugh at her like they did at school. Mother had made her wear the glasses again, saying contact lenses were silly and not good for her. She hid the contact lenses; she didn't throw them away as Mother had told her to do. Mother was right, she was a wilful child.

She was on this train because her mother had found the card and Jane confessed to seeing Phillip. Mother said she would make sure that Jane never spoke him or any man again. Men, as Mother said, always hurt women and leave them. She knew that meant she would never be allowed to talk to Dr Manse or see him again.

Her mother was right, Dr Manse had acted inappropriately by holding her hand and taking her to places in the town. He had cuddled her when she got upset and showed her how pretty she was in a mirror. He was nice and she had wanted to be with him. Dr Manse loved her, and wanted to help her. He would find a flat in London where they could live and he was going to show her all the sites of London and he was going to make her very happy. She wanted to go out again, to enjoy the sunshine, to have people look at her like she was an adult and not a simple child looked after by her mother. She wanted to sit on a train again with real people and be normal.

Mother wouldn't let her leave. Mother wanted to lock her in her room. She had to stop mother screaming at her and making her unhappy. She kept the bloody knife in her bag wrapped in her best handkerchief. She would show it to Dr Manse when she arrived in London. Mother was quiet now and Jane was glad of that. She took the purse from her mother's bag and the card with Phillip's address on it. She had enough money to get her to London. She placed her mother on the settee to rest and turned on the television so Mother had something to watch and didn't get bored. She said goodbye and her mother stared unblinking into space.

Mother was always right, she really was a very wilful, naughty girl.

Those watching her saw a very slight smile appear on her face and wondered if she was thinking nice thoughts.

THE GRASS IS GREENER

He was just 17 years old and he was beginning to feel a little scared. He had never been to London; he lived his life in Portsmouth but today he was going to make his fortune in London. He was a good-looking lad with a jaunty quiff which showed off his blond, thick hair. Some might have surmised he was a choir boy from his fresh-faced innocent look but they would have been mistaken. Robert Charles Halliday, known to his friends as "Robbie the Robber" because he had a reputation for stealing anything he could lay his hands on, was proud of the title and worked hard to maintain it. His talent was thwarted many times by the police but up to now he had only a few conditional cautions and a couple of referral orders; nothing much to worry about. With all the youth-offending teams working to help him make better decisions, they had helped him get his CSCS card so he could work on building sites. He didn't know what he wanted to do but at least he could earn some money quite easily just being a goffer on sites if he wanted. They had also helped him create a CV, so armed with his CSCS card and a CV he was off to London to make his fortune.

Sitting on the train that had stopped now for ages, he was beginning to get a bit jittery. *Had he thought this through? Perhaps he should have waited a bit longer?* All this waiting was not doing him any good. He had to leave his home. His stepfather was continually on at him and he had had enough. The man was psychotic; all he kept saying was go to college and get qualifications and then a proper job. He was like a broken record and never left him alone. He, Robert Charles Halliday, knew better than that bastard. Although his reputation of Robbie the Robber was a good one, he had embarked on another earner. He smoked a bit of weed but nothing too much and he was approached to sell weed and other stuff which was a good earner. Why have a job when you can earn twice as much selling stuff? It's a no-brainer. Well, he had been doing quite nicely. He had lots of contacts through being known as Robbie the Robber and was making about £200 per day and more. He had been selling for about six months and was, perhaps, a little too obvious in acquiring designer stuff, he conceded. With this stash of drug cash he could buy the latest phone, the best trainers and clothes and even a bit of jewellery. His stepfather had begun to notice all the fancy clothes and jewellery; he was no fool and knew where it had come from. He took Robert to one side and warned him that he was going to tell the police if he didn't stop selling drugs and told him he had to get a proper job or else. Well, the argument wasn't nice and it turned a little violent. Robert carried a knife because you have to if you are carrying drugs to sell, it's protection, it's not rocket science is it? In the heat of the moment, he pulled out his knife and threatened his stepfather. He saw in a moment the look of fear in his stepfather's eyes but that quickly got replaced by anger. He was told to get out and not come back. In temper, Robert told his stepfather that he wouldn't stay in the house with such a bastard and he was off to London to make his fortune and that he would make more money in a week than him, a sad loser, than his stepfather could earn in a year. Neither could trust themselves not to get into a physical fight so the stepfather left the house in a flurry of temper and bile and Robert went to his room to pack, hating the bastard for interfering in his life. He reckoned when he got to London he could make even more money, London was a big place. Once he got a bit of a job and was settled, he would get organised and have a good life. He would show his stepfather that he knew what he was doing and had made a success of everything and how he was not only be richer than his stepfather who was a piddling civil servant working in the townhall doing piddling jobs but he would be powerful too.

Now the train had stopped for so long he wondered if perhaps he had been a little rash. Would he know how to sell in London? He had good contacts in Portsmouth. Where would he live? He had nowhere to stay in London. He didn't know how you find a place to stay in London. He had some money but not a lot. He tended to spend his money when he got it. He had always had the safety of his home and now he had nowhere to go. He felt that cold chill of fear of the unknown. He couldn't go back. He nearly stabbed his stepfather. In the heat of the argument, he shocked himself by threatening the man with his knife. He didn't think he would ever use it. The knife was there to only scare people. He would never be forgiven at home, but then in defiance he thought the bastard deserved to be scared, he never left him alone. Always moaning about him, telling him what to do, never satisfied by anything he did. In thinking about him again he thought in temper and disgust, *I wish I had stabbed him, that would teach him a lesson.*

So, he had packed his designer Gucci black rucksack; it had cost him a fortune, actually £1,590 and he hadn't needed it but it looked good and it impressed everyone so it did the job. Now he needed it to fill with a few bits of clothes. He packed some weed too which would be his little bit of pleasure and some to sell if able. As a seller of weed and stuff, you never know when you can make a sale. He thought he was rather good at selling. He hoped that would continue in London. Sitting there in silence, the train not moving, he wondered again where he would sleep tonight. He reckoned if push came to shove, he could sleep on the station. Tomorrow he could look for somewhere to stay and look for a building site to work on until he got settled. Obviously, he wanted to go back to selling weed and stuff. London was full of druggies, and he reckoned it would be easy to sell there and he would make even more money than in Portsmouth. He would show the bastard how successful he was going to be.

The bonus was he wasn't known in London by the police. They were getting a bit nosey in Portsmouth and they seemed to be watching him more than he would have liked. He was pretty nifty and could escape their search for him but he knew eventually they would get him. But in London it was new territory. The police didn't know him and he could walk about and do what he liked. He was after all Robbie the Robber and very versatile. He was skilful at stealing from shops and London was full of them he told himself smugly. He didn't mind a bit of pickpocketing stuff; he was better at it than anyone he knew. Housebreaking was an option, he had done that a few times but you need to know the area and who lived where; he would have to learn that in London. There was so much he could do to start with to make money. He smiled: life would be much better in London once he got settled. He just needed to find somewhere to sleep, at the moment that was his main worry.

The lady sitting opposite Robert had been watching him through hooded eyes. She could see he was struggling and then seemed to perk up. He was by himself and he looked quite young. She was well aware of young people and his looks were gorgeous, yes, he could be taken for a 14-year-old but she reckoned from his hands and attitude he was nearer 17 or 18 years old. He didn't look too tall either, he was sitting down so she thought maybe 5' 6" tall. This would make him perfect. She was used to runaways. London got so many young people who arrived with nowhere to live and full of immature and unachievable hopes and dreams. She sighed, they never seemed to learn. London was not an easy place to live in without money or contacts.

Vanessa Elizabeth Bentall was a very nice-looking woman of 45 years old. She had worn well in a sophisticated way. Her clothes were good quality and fashionable. The look of them said Regent Street and Mayfair, more designer than chain stores. Her hair was black and bold with a short but stylish style which complemented her bold red lipstick. She was a stunner but Robert was too engrossed to notice. He was still wondering where he would sleep tonight and where he would eat; he was beginning to feel hungry and wondered if there was a buffet car where he could get something to fill the gap. He saw the woman looking at him and, embarrassed at first, then with a smile he asked politely if she knew if there was a buffet car on this train.

"Are you hungry or thirsty?" she asked.

"Both," he replied with a rueful smile.

She smiled back and said she knew there was a buffet car and she would get him a drink and a sandwich. He tried to argue that he could get it but she smiled and graciously leant across and tapped his hand and told him to behave and she was happy to get it. Her last comment before she walked to the buffet car was, "Is it a Pepsi you would like?"

He nodded and mumbled, "Thank you."

Vanessa came back armed with sandwiches, crisps and a couple of bananas; there was a coffee for her and a Pepsi for him. She sat down with a sigh and watched him eat the two sandwiches with relish and speed; one sandwich was beef and one was cheese. He hadn't realised just how hungry he was and they were so tasty. The Pepsi hit the spot too and when he had finished, he tried to offer money to Vanessa but she smiled and told him to put the notes away. She was happy to do it. He thought she was an angel and he felt so lucky to have met her. She asked him where he was going and sat back and waited for his response full of lies and unrealistic expectations.

He told her he was going to get work on a building site. She asked kindly if he had enough money until then. She pointed out that he would have to work for a week before he would get paid. Robert nodded and said he was OK. He hadn't thought of that and he wondered if he would be OK. When she asked where he was going to stay, Robert squirmed a little and stuttered that he thought he had an aunt who lived somewhere in London he was going to contact. She knew that was a lie. She smiled benignly and he thought she was wonderful and so very kind. It had actually been a long time since anyone had bothered to be kind to him. He knew he had a reputation of being a hard man to his clients and friends and his mother and stepfather thought he was a belligerent, argumentative bastard but he liked being treated so nicely, it warmed him and he realised he missed affection.

She could see he liked her words and wanted to please him further. She knew he thought of himself as a tough big lad and she reckoned he thought himself a big fish in his area but he was a big fish in a tiny pool, London fish would eat him up. She smiled again and told him she ran a boarding house. She added it wasn't fancy, just a big house with big rooms but she let the rooms out to help her with her bills. He sat up a bit straighter. She could see this bit of information was of interest. Careful not to sound too controlling, she pursed her lips as if she was thinking and added hesitantly, "I have one small room still vacant. I usually don't rent that out, I have to say. It's quite small but it has a bed and wardrobe and TV in it if you are at all interested. I just feel a little concerned that you are new to London and maybe need a few weeks to get settled. You could then move on to a bigger flat when you are more settled."

She added for gravitas, "My two sons have now moved to Australia, so it's nice to have people living in my house. It's sort of company."

Robert couldn't believe his luck. This angel of a woman

was going to help him. The only thing that was worrying him was somewhere to sleep and that was sorted. The relief overwhelmed him. He actually hadn't realised just how worried he had been. She told him to call her Mrs Smith, no need to tell him her real name, not necessary. He profusely thanked her and couldn't hide his pleasure at having met such a wonderful angel and someone who would help him in London.

Vanessa, used to strays and waifs, carried on smiling while she considered the benefits of this young lad. She had many male clients waiting for a young blond lad who looked like he was a choir boy. She would earn a lot of money through him. She reckoned she would dress him in younger clothes and take off all his jewellery. Maybe a little eye make up to make his eyes bigger, they were so blue and it would make them look more innocent. Normally she walked around the big London stations looking for young lads who had left home. Some were so deep in drugs they couldn't function and their skins were badly marked but this lad fell into her lap so to speak on a train and he was perfect; beautiful skin, light on drugs, slim and quite charming. She would earn a fortune from him.

The train had started with a jolt and they were on their way to London. Both Robert and Vanessa couldn't wait to arrive. They both thought they had hit the jackpot and life would be good. The smug smiles on both their faces lasted all the way to London.

THE RED BERET

He sat ramrod straight on the train, he looked straight ahead and didn't waiver. He could see out of the corner of his eye the interest from other passengers. Those looking at him thought he looked most uncomfortable but Sergeant Jack Phillips was used to it; training made him able to sit for hours, straight and not moving. In full ceremonial uniform of the paras, he knew he looked good. But he was hiding a secret. He didn't deserve to be in this proud uniform.

The train had stopped now for at least an hour and it seemed to give him time to reflect and think, something he hadn't done for a long time. He realised he had joined the army for all the wrong reasons. At school and college, he was athletic and strong. He was a sprinter and could run faster than anyone else in his college and he won all club events. He was good at everything, especially in the football team where he helped his school win many trophies. Joining the army seemed a good way forward and he loved the training. Every aspect of it: climbing, running, crawling, he was the best. He was soon made a corporal on the back of his athletic skills and he took pride in who he was. He felt the kingpin in his battalion where others were exhausted and wanting to lie down after training, he, Jack Phillips, could go out again and run the course. He never ran out of energy and was cited by his Commanding Officer as an outstanding soldier and became the benchmark for all soldiers in the training camp.

When his battalion left training to embark on their journey to Afghanistan, Jack was kept behind. It was recognised that he was such a good example of a trained soldier, they promoted him to sergeant and he helped with the new influx of soldiers. For two years he never saw any fields of battle and this suited him very well. He was an athlete and he won everything. He was encouraged to enter all sorts of events through the Army, which he won and he was training for the Olympics. Life was good and he got a bit complacent and maybe a little cocky, he conceded. It's tough to be top of the pile and praised by everyone. He smiled a little at that ironic thought.

So, it came as a shock, after two years of training, to be told he was being sent to Afghanistan to join his battalion. There had been some fatalities and injuries and he was needed to join them. Although he had no experience of frontline work, he was considered a capable para with two years' experience. Under his breath he said, *bloody army top nobs know nothing*. He remembered he had argued with his Commanding Officer stating his work in helping with the training of new recruits had to be more important. He reminded them that he was training for the Olympics, that the paras won every Army contest in athletics and football because of him. He stopped trying to convince his Commanding Officer when he noted he was getting nowhere and was now sounding like a whining child. He was shit-scared. He did not want to experience the theatre of war as the paras like to call frontline conflicts. He had joined the bloody paras for the training not to go to war. *How pathetic and stupid am I to think it would never happen?* he thought. He was everything a good soldier should be: tall, fit and with knowledge that made him a potential killing machine. But he hated the thought of killing anyone and the noise of the guns and bombs sent shivers of panic through him. He coped in training because he knew they wouldn't kill him but in Afghanistan they were all there to bloody kill him. He didn't want to go.

He packed up and was to go on the next available flight. He was shipped out that evening. The army didn't mess around. His arrival was what he expected. He had heard from returning paras what a hellhole it was. The heat hit him first, then the sand that just got everywhere but it was never knowing what was around the corner, who might be behind the door or window that caused a tenseness everyone experienced. You had to be on your guard the whole time; even in your guarded encampment. Most he noticed coped well and the jokes were banded around during meal times and recreation times. But Jack was tense with fear and trepidation. He hated it there and wanted to go home. He was surrounded by intense macho men and could never reveal how he felt. He was a bloody sergeant, so in charge of a group of brave, highly trained men. He blustered and shouted and gave off so much testosterone that everyone thought he was John Wayne. He smiled at the thought now. Looking back in the safety of a train in England made his thoughts easier.

It was that day, it was going to happen at some point, he knew that. They had got up at 6a.m. as usual and were geared up for a routine search of the nearby town that was now just a wreck of partly blown-up homes and glassless windows. The inhabitants had long left and found other places to live. It was the weirdest place to be. There was no sound except the wind whipping up little myriads of dust that swirled noiselessly around the bricks and mortar that once were homes. Although the place was lifeless, Jack and his men knew there could be guns trained on them from behind the stark walls or a mine placed in the ground for them to tread on. The enemy waited there with mortars and marksmen waiting for the supply trucks that had to pass through. The area was regularly cleared and mines were disarmed or marked. It was a filthy job and Jack never knew what was waiting for him and his men. So far, there hadn't been much trouble; the odd gunman or two that his team easily dispensed with. He kept telling himself, *They were the paras and they were good*. It didn't make him feel any better.

This day was especially hot and in full combat clothing, it felt like a sauna. The quiet of the town seemed spooky today and it seemed like they all felt this as they looked around and with stealth worked together in a tried-and-tested manner checking each building and looking for mines. A golden eagle swooped down and Jack caught a glimpse of its dark brown body as a spooked para shot it thinking it was a drone. It felt wrong today. He signalled to his men, scattered lightly around him, to calm down and to head for one of the larger homes off the main road. He would give them instructions on how they were going to work today.

There were eight of them and himself now in what was once someone's home and now looked like a demolition site. They took the opportunity to drink some water whilst Jack gave orders on the search. The first bullets to hit the house shook the building and dust flew everywhere. Each man scrambled for a window to fight back. Jack using his field glasses spotted something shining out of a house about two hundred metres away. It sounded like and he could see a little of the weapon and reckoned it was a DShK Heavy Machine Gun. Intelligence had told him that this was the preferred weapon the Taliban had appropriated from the Soviet Union. It was bloody devastating. His men couldn't move from their position or retaliate because the fire kept coming. After about two minutes there was a short break but not long enough to get to another building. All his men could do was fire back but in no time the machine gun started again and they all had to lay low as the bullets pierced the barely standing walls. He could see the walls would give way soon, holes were appearing and getting bigger in the tired and sandy bricks, it wouldn't be long before any cover would be gone and they would be picked off as sitting ducks.

Jack, ignoring his pounding heart and damping down the fear that kept rising into his throat, had to come up with a solution. His men looked to him to get them out of the situation. It was then that he realised all the years of training and skill were needed now. He told his men to stay put. He dropped his gun, took of his helmet, and started to undress. The jacket was heavy and full of materials he didn't need at the moment. The body protection wasn't needed and he stood in trousers and vest and boots. In his hands he carried two hand grenades; he was ready. He told his men to watch and wait and to fire at the machine gun to give him cover. No one else could move as fast as he could and he knew he was their only chance of surviving this.

Dripping with a fearful sweat, Jack took a deep breath and crawled near to the open space that once was a door. The incessant deafening explosion of bullets hitting the walls caused the air to fill with dirt and dust choking him. Then it stopped. It was, hopefully, a two-minute window and Jack was taking this time to move. His passing comment as he charged out into the open space was, "Cover me with fire but make sure you don't bloody shoot me!"

He sprinted like he had never sprinted before. His feet felt like they were running on air. He hardly breathed as he pushed himself with a force and determination that no competition had engendered in him. He ran faster than time, than life itself. He had to get to the small shed one hundred metres away. The Taliban would have seen him and he hoped and prayed his men would keep a line of fire going to stop the terrorists lining up their guns to drop him dead.

He reached the small shed and dropped to the floor gasping for air. He was told later that the soldiers had never seen anyone run so fast and they reckoned he would have smashed the world record. Shaking with adrenalin and fear, Jack curled up in a small ball as the bullets hit the small shed and the area around it. How none of the bullets got him, he never knew. His men were now able to fire continuously at the area and keep the Taliban unable to do nothing but fire the damned machine gun. Deafened by the noise, Jack put his hands over his ears and waited what seemed an eternity for the break to happen.

Again, silence, and Jack fired up on so much adrenalin, jumped up and hearing his men continuously firing at the machine-gun area, took a deep breath and ran the last one hundred yards towards the machine gun. He had no idea how many men were in there but he had two grenades and if he could get close enough, it would do the trick. This run was so dangerous and Jack was in the open and an easy target; he ran like he had never run before. He heard nothing, he felt nothing, he just flew. He felt like the golden eagle he had seen. He was swooping and the rush he felt was the air parting in deference ahead of him. The bullet that hit him didn't seem to stop him. He was invincible and he carried on. The second bullet to hit him grazed his ear, he couldn't feel it but he heard it. He had reached the house with the machine gun and the third bullet floored him as it pierced his chest. Laying on the floor something uncanny happened. Jack could feel nothing but he knew he was alive. He crawled the last 5 yards, close enough now to throw the grenades. He pulled the pin and threw the grenade with all his might into the open gap and quickly did the same with the second grenade. He curled up in a ball, pretty sure he was done for now and prayed.

The explosion was enormous, the grenades had not only exploded but there were also other inflammables in the abandoned house and the lot went up. Jack, choked with shrapnel and bricks and dust and sand invading his body and striking him from all angles. When the noise stopped, Jack hadn't realised he had gone deaf and could hear nothing. But he felt a searing and intense pain in every orifice and every part of his body. The job was done and if he could have, he would have smiled. The abandoned house was now a pile of rubble with a twisted torn metal which had been a machine gun. They said that there were six Taliban in there, all dead now.

His men found Jack, just about alive, under a heap of bricks and dust and dragged him back to their encampment. An armoured truck had been sent for and Jack remembered every bump as the truck rushed them back. He was moved back to England after initial medical help but he was told he needed to go home for various operations and recuperation. He didn't argue. The Post Traumatic Stress Disorder as it was called kicked in after the operations had successfully removed bullets and shrapnel that had embedded themselves around his body. The night sweats and the reliving of the event kept him awake most nights. He had never in his whole life known fear like he did on that fateful day and his PTSD was all about his fear.

His men had feted him as an absolute hero and were telling everyone how he had saved their lives. That if it wasn't for him, they would have died. That he ran so fast no one could believe anyone could run that fast. His Commanding Officer said he deserved a medal for what he did. Jack couldn't tell them. He was a coward, he hated what he had to do. He didn't want to be in a war and he didn't want to kill anyone and now he would pay the price for what looked like bravery but was actually just the inevitable choice. He was the only one who could have done it.

He would never go to war again. His injuries were such that he walked with a limp and he would never run again, the bullet had pierced his lung and his breathing was laboured. They were sending him to London for more treatment. He was grateful for that but he really didn't want to go to the next bit.

The Palace had sent him a letter inviting him to receive a medal. They were going to give him the Victoria Cross along with other heroes. The Victoria Cross was the highest and most prestigious award of the British honours system. It was awarded for valour "in the presence of the enemy" to members of the British Armed Forces. To received such a momentous honour was screwing him up. He was no hero, he was a coward, he had been shit-scared and didn't deserve to breath the same air of real heroes.

But he had to accept it for his battalion who were going to have a party afterwards to celebrate. They called him a hero; they loved him for what he had done. His only choice was to receive the medal for his men. He woke up dripping in sweat, crying and shaking most nights, reliving the moment he ran for his life. He remembered the fear and panic he felt and that had made him run faster than he had ever run. He could never tell anyone of the fear he felt. *God!!* he thought, *I don't deserve the honour; I am not worthy.* It was his torment and his lie he would always have to live with.

THE SPEECH

"For goodness sake, woman!! Where the bloody hell is my shirt." He was getting very agitated and she could see he would get red in the face and start sweating and they both knew that wasn't good.

"Jamie, it's here," she said, holding up a perfectly ironed and starched white shirt.

"How many times do I have to tell you my name is James not Jamie. I am James Arthur Dooley and that's how I want to be addressed."

She giggled. "Oh my dear, stop it. I can't call you James Arthur Dooley every time I speak to you, that's silly."

He was getting beyond angry now.

"For God's sake, Jennifer!!! How many times have I said I am not called 'my dear'. I want you to say 'my darling', it's so much more in keeping with our station."

He started his usual tirade of *How will anyone take me seriously if my wife doesn't respect me. When we go out, I need you to keep up with how we are now living, we have standards to maintain.*

She thought that he never came out with her so no

one would notice anyway. They never went anywhere, not even to the shops together. But she smiled and apologised. She thought him silly but it was all very important to him and she would support him as best she could.

Today was a very special day for him. He was going to be made Master of the Club. Something he had worked so hard to achieve for years now. He knew she would never understand this. He had married a sweet, innocent utterly stupid woman all those years ago and now he was making something of himself he was landed with her – she was stupid and common and just didn't understand how important he had become.

Jennifer Dooley was happy with her lot in life. She had married Jamie when they were late teens. They had giggled and loved and built a home for themselves. Children hadn't happened and she hadn't gone to work. Jamie thought it beneath him to have a working wife. He actually wanted her to join the local women's clubs *and make something of herself* as he put it. But she wasn't interested in that. She had gone along to the local WI Club but the women there were not her type. They were snobby and looked down on her and it wasn't fun so she stopped going. She was very happy at home cooking and cleaning and gardening. She had a nice life. Jamie was doing well at work and had been made a manager in the plumbing yard he worked at. He was proud of his achievement. She had never gone to his place of work. Jamie thought it inappropriate for wives to venture into men's territory. *Work was work and home was home* was Jamie's saying. She would have liked to meet his colleagues but it wasn't going to happen.

Four years ago, Jamie joined this men's-only club. She wasn't even sure what it was called. Every time she tried to talk about it he said it was a men's club and you just didn't discuss it with anyone outside of the club. It kept him very happy and he would go there twice a week. The only thing she knew was that she didn't have to cook for him on those nights and he liked a clean white shirt, starched and ironed for those evenings. She didn't mind him going out in the evening because he seemed very happy and proud to be part of it. She had her programmes on the telly and when he was out she could watch what she wanted to. She loved the soaps and any reality shows, they made her laugh.

Jamie, he had a lot on his mind at the moment with his job as manager and now he was going to be made master of his club. She knew he had worked so hard to achieve this. She had never met anyone from the club, apparently women were not allowed to be in it, but he talked about how well he was doing there and how they thought he was marvellous and clever and such a good organiser. He was very proud of his achievement.

She knew he was ashamed of her. Jamie had taken to speaking *proper*. He had tried to get Jennifer to speak better but she wouldn't have any of it. She told him many, many times that she was who she was. They had both lived in Barking, Essex and had the local East London/Essex twang and there was nothing wrong with that, she had told him. They had been neighbours and went to school together and eventually married. Their parents were good people she had reminded him. He seemed ashamed of them too. Her dad worked for the council on the bins and his dad was a parks gardener. They had moved away not long after they got married because Jamie said he wanted a better start in life and he got a good job with the plumbing company in Hampshire.

Jennifer missed her family but wasn't bored with her life. Jamie was adamant she wouldn't go to work so she kept busy in the house and garden. He said a man of his station in life didn't have a wife that worked. He was getting more and more of a *toff* as she called him but never to his face.

It shows how busy he had been because it seemed to Jennifer that it had been ages since they had actually spent any time together. Well, they ate together except when he was out, and sometimes he worked late if there was something urgent to do in his job, she knew how particular he was. He always said he wanted to reach the top of his job and was looking to be made a director in years to come. When Jamie told her this she laughed. *A director?* She thought. *He really fancied himself,* but it upset him a lot so she didn't laugh again. He was very ambitious.

So tonight was very, very important. He was being made master; the highest honour you can get in the club he told her. She said she would have liked to watch him but he said no she wouldn't be allowed there as no women were allowed in. She accepted this and kissed him on the head and said how proud she was of him. He blustered and said he hoped she hadn't put lipstick anywhere near his collar. She laughed and said she wasn't wearing any so he was safe. He had his new suit as well for the occasion.

He had been working on his speech for months. He read some of it to her and she clapped him at being so brilliant. He sounded very statesman-like and she told him how proud she was of him. He liked that and smiled. The speech he said was his crowning glory and would make his master-ship perfect. As he said, he needed to show them that a man from humble beginnings could ascend to the heady heights of being made master. He also hinted, none too subtlety to Jennifer, that this might help him reach his goal as a director of the plumbing company. He whispered that being master of this organisation was considered a stepping stone to greater things in someone's working life.

The speech was the driving force in his life. He bought a dictionary to look up big words he had never used to put in it to impress. Jennifer knew how important this speech was for him. She looked in the dictionary for hours, trawling words that might be good for him to use. She found a brilliant one: *colloquy,* meaning conversation, talk. It was fucking fantastic! She blushed. Although he wasn't around, he didn't like her swearing and said it was common. But realising she was alone in the house and feeling happy and impish, she shouted out, "I found a fucking brilliant word for you, Jamie, my dear." She laughed feeling really good.

That evening when he got home, she rushed to show him the word she had found for him. Excited and glad to be helping, she shoved the dictionary under his nose and said, "Look, that one, it's f… flipping brilliant." She remembered not to swear.

He looked and then looked at her surprised. "So who showed you this?" he asked. She sensed an underlying menace in his voice.

Faltering a little, not knowing how to react, she quietly said, "No, I found it. I, I looked through each page for ages trying to find you a good word to use." She looked into his eyes and asked, "Are you angry with me?"

He seemed to relax for a moment and with a sigh stated, "No, of course not. It's just it's not going to fit into my speech but thanks anyway. What's for dinner?"

After dinner he went to his study, the small bedroom was now called the study. Actually, he liked the word and spent the evening looking to put it into his speech.

Jennifer again asked if she might meet some of his colleagues. As she said, if he was to reach such heady heights, shouldn't the wife be introduced. She just wanted to meet some of the people he always talked about with great reverence. Again, he said no. *Work was work and home was home, never the two would meet.* She asked if all the wives were the same in the club and at his work. He assured her no women were allowed in either area. Jennifer accepted this and laughed that perhaps that was good because she knew nothing about his club or his work and would look a bit silly if she met them. He laughed and agreed.

But she had to admit the speech had taken its toll on their evenings. When Jamie had been in, he went straight to the spare room he now called his study. He would sit in there for hours writing and rewriting his speech. It was going to be the best and most important speech in his career and life. Writing the speech had taken months to prepare. It was now ready and he was very proud of it. No, he had said, he couldn't read it all to her because it had private bits that pertain to the club only. The bits he had read to her were the only parts she could know of.

He was so proud and pleased with his speech. It made him sound statesman-like and very masterful. It was full of words he had never used and voiced sentiments he had read about. He was going to be the best master ever in the club. The speech was four pages full of amazing facts and he had trawled many books to find an appropriate joke to put in too. He knew it was fantastic.

Unbeknown to Jennifer, he had invited his boss and wife to the evening to show off his new position and his ability to give a good speech of acceptance as master. He also invited the directors of his company and their wives too hoping that would show them how important he had become. Tonight was going to be his Waterloo, his Premiership, his success.

He had suggested Jennifer catch the 4.30p.m. train to London and stay with her parents for a few days. He said he was going to be very busy as master in the first few days and he worried she would be alone. Jennifer thought this strange because she had been alone for many months whilst the speech had been written. Going home for a few days suited her. She had lots to tell her parents and looked forward to seeing them. Packed and nearly ready to go, Jennifer suggested Jamie might want to buy a bottle of something nice to have in the house when he got back. A brandy or whisky because he would deserve a drink after the evening. He thought that really nice of her to think of that. While she finished getting ready, he popped out to the local supermarket.

She shouldn't have done it. But all the secrecy had got to her. She wanted to read the speech. She deserved to see it. It had taken so much time and left her alone so many evenings, she felt she was part of it. Once she heard the door close as he left, she rushed upstairs to the spare room/study. There on the table was The Speech, beautifully laid out on the small table. He had got it typed by someone, the letters were in a good-looking font and set out in double spacing and it looked proper. She was too scared to pick up the pages, they were so clean and pristine and he would know she had touched them. It did look so professional and she knew he would be so proud to hold those pages and give his speech tonight. She knew he was clever; she knew he was ambitious and wanted to do well in life. He was going to be a great success. With a sigh she left the spare room/study and picked up her bag and coat. She had a train to catch and it was getting late.

The train had stopped for an hour now. The passengers in the carriage were getting restless. The train had been going for only half an hour and it stopped with no sign of it starting yet. Bored and fed up, each passenger looked furtively around the carriage at their fellow passengers. It seemed all eyes were locked on the woman sitting by herself next to the window. They noticed she seemed to change from floods of quiet tears to muttering under her breath with a look of anger. She kept her head down but every time she searched for a hankie in her bag and coat, she glanced to see if anyone was looking at her. All eyes moved quickly away but returned after a few minutes. They all wondered what had happened to her to make her cry in public.

Jennifer couldn't help it. She now had time to think, sitting here waiting for the bloody train to start again. She had time on her hands and wanted to go over everything that had happened this afternoon. When she went into the spare room/bloody study as he called it – tosser!! She called him. She had read the first page without touching the paper. It began by saying something about his good wife not being well and unable to attend tonight. He welcomed all the men and women to the evening. Women? Women were invited too? After the initial shock, and just to be quite sure, she read the treacherous lines again, it was unbelievable, how could he do this to her, and why would he do this to her? She asked herself. She knew in her heart of hearts he was ashamed of her, wanting her to speak properly, dress better and use *lah-di-dah* language like *oh my darling*, like he wanted her to but this, this awfulness of lying and keeping her in the house and out of sight was just too much to take in. The hurt, the righteous indignation and the absolutely white heat of an anger she had never experienced before had overtaken her and left her breathless. The bastard!! Time was getting on and she had to go and catch the train and then think it all through.

Upset and hurt she may have been but she was not stupid. With a smile that had maleficent written all over it, she picked up the hallowed speech, the make-or-break-me speech, the fucking awesome speech that was going to make him a director speech and stuffed it in her bag.

Here she was sitting on the train going to London and it had stopped for an hour now. She knew everyone in the carriage was watching her and she could see looks of pity on their faces as she wiped away tears. What they didn't know was the tears were not of sadness, more, tears of anger and frustration and wanting revenge. She had been a good wife. She knew she was not what he wanted but she loved him and cared for him and this was her reward. He was a stuck-up arsehole and she was fed up with his pretend middle-class attitude. He was as common as muck, like her, and she knew everyone else could see it too, he didn't fool anyone – the prick!

To while away the time she had read the speech in full. *The speech is fucking boring, and he is an asshole*, she thought and she saw he had used her *colloquy* word too, he couldn't even give her credit for finding him a fucking word. So, on her way to London now with the speech in her bag, she wondered how the hell he was going to amaze everyone tonight. She reckoned, knowing him, he would just panic and not be able to say a word. That would look good to all his bastard friends; wouldn't it? Oh she would have loved to have watched his total humiliation. He would be finished after tonight. He was not someone who could ad-lib – he wasn't that clever. Everyone would see he was a tinpot cretin with no brains at all. He would be finished.

In her bag she had the credit card, which was in their joint names but he always kept it, he said she didn't need it. She found it in his bedside cabinet and took it. Tomorrow she intended to max it out. The join-account card she had for shopping would be emptied too. She was looking forward now to going home to Barking. She missed her life there. Oh life will be good now and to cheer herself up she just envisaged his face when he got back to find his speech was missing with only a couple of hours before the big event. Oh revenge is so, so sweet. Those in the carriage looked up surprised to see her giggling now.

THE WATCH

The train had stopped now for what was ages and everyone was getting fed up and restless. The girl across the aisle seemed worth watching as she smiled and grimaced to herself. She looked deep in thought and seemed to be remembering nice things and not so nice things. Passengers thought she was quite interesting during this dull and boring time. Of course, no one talked to each other, most tried to read their books or magazines or newspapers but some, those with nothing better to do, just idled and surmised what this girl was thinking about.

Joni Mitchell was her name. She had been named after some singer years ago that her parents liked. When she was younger and more susceptible to lies, she believed that she was related to the Joni Mitchell who wrote and sang songs about social and philosophical ideals and things like that. She was famous and Joni mark 2 as she was called, boasted well into her teens that she was related to this wonderful and talented woman. It came as a humiliating shock when she was laughingly told by her parents that it was just a bit of fun, that she wasn't related at all to Joni the singer. Joni mark 2 had built her friendships and relationships on the fact she was related to Joni Mitchell and she made her parents promise never to tell anyone anything different. So, Joni Mitchell from Portsmouth made it known that she was related to Joni Mitchell the singer and for ever that is what would be told.

Living a lie isn't easy for anyone Joni thought. She had researched the singer Joni Mitchell because friends and acquaintances had annoyingly asked questions about her. Truthfully Joni said she had never met her because she lived in Canada and wasn't well anymore but she added falsely that her parents had been to Canada many years ago and obviously stayed with the singer and got the best seats at her concerts. When you live a lie for many years you begin to believe it. Joni Mitchell had an entitled, stuck-up and diva-ish attitude that didn't make her very popular and the friends and acquaintances had over time disappeared.

Joni was a good-looking girl with long, dark brown, thick hair that shone on her shoulders and framed her heart-shaped face. She was now 25 years old and when she smiled her face lit up and attracted most of the local men in town. Life had been interesting and she had many boyfriends so the lack of girlfriends didn't really worry her at all. When one boy left and they never stayed long, there was always another.

She was employed in an office to type and file and do whatever was wanted. It was boring but she would regale to all present her history and her knowledge of Joni Mitchell which seemed to impress quite a few of the girls she worked with. But Joni never stayed in a job very long. She got bored and the girls would start to pick on her. She thought because they were jealous of her being related to Joni Mitchell. They couldn't cope with it. They were always picking on her saying things had been stolen and they blamed her. It was just so unfair. Office jobs were easy to get so Joni, not wishing to put up with such jealousy, would leave and go somewhere else. Portsmouth had lots of offices spread around the town.

Her latest job was the worst though. She had no idea that women could be quite so bitchy and jealous and she hated them. She got a new job with a shipping merchant. It was a busy and seemed a fun place to work. The girls were friendly and often they all went out for lunch on a Friday to celebrate the coming weekend. Everything had been fine for the first three months and then it started.

Money had started to go missing from the girls' bags. Nothing very much, a few pounds at a time but this seemed to be happening regularly. Girls being girls, they started to panic and accuse each other and it got so uncomfortable that Mr Green, the boss, had to interject. He saw each girl individually to find out what had happened, how much taken and when. Mr Green thought he could be a detective and sort this out. Strangely the only girl to not lose anything was Joni but as Joni told Mr Green, she always carried her bag with her and she wasn't stupid like the other girls who never watched their belongings. Mr Green agreed she was very sensible.

From then on every girl in the office carried her bag everywhere with her and they all eyed each other up with distrust. There was a thief amongst them and the happy-go-lucky atmosphere had gone and a black cloud hung over the office. When she started the job, she told the stories about Joni Mitchell the singer being her relative which had everyone in awe of her being related to someone famous. But now when she talked about Joni the singer eyes would roll up to the ceiling and the girls would mutter with distain, "Not again, just fuck off!!" This was very upsetting to Joni.

A further month down the line saw the girls gradually going back to their normal usual happy selves and trust seemed to have reappeared. Nothing had been stolen and everyone was feeling better and more amenable. Joni was feeling more comfortable. This time theft from bags was minimal and some girls were not sure if they were missing a pound coin or not so didn't mention it. Small things seemed to disappear like a comb or a lipstick and most of the girls wondered if they had misplaced them, lost them or just forgotten to bring them in. The catalyst was Betty May's watch.

Now Betty May's watch was something else. Betty May had a boyfriend who was rather well off and absolutely adored Betty May. He bought her lots of presents which Betty May brought in and showed to the girls. This latest present was the best and Betty May whispered reverently, "This is a Swarovski Cocktail watch and it cost," she lowered her voice even more and almost mouthed slowly and firmly, "two hundred and eighty pounds." The gasp from all could be heard in the next room. The beautiful, elegant watch was viewed closely. The rectangular face was nestled in the wrist band of links that were rosegold with what looked like alternating bejewelled links. Someone spotted the Swarovski swan above the twelve o'clock on the black watch face and they could all see how expensive it was with the designer logo. Joni wasn't impressed and didn't like Betty May; she thought she was very boastful.

It was nearly 5.30p.m. and everyone was beginning to get ready to go home. It had been an easy day and everyone was chatting about what they were doing that evening. It was about then that the shriek was heard, followed by a scream. They rushed to the toilets where the scream came from and found Betty May sobbing. She called out, "My lovely watch, it's gone. I can't find it anywhere." Mr Green came out of his office to enquire what the heck was happening and was confronted by a group of girls trying to manoeuvre an almost collapsed Betty May into the office and sit her down.

Joni was part of the crowd of girls trying to help Betty May but to be quite honest, she was disgusted by the pathetic fuss being made over a watch. Joni had never experienced such a distasteful mass hysteria like this. Obviously, Mr Green had because he took charge and calmed everyone down and ordered coffee to be brought in from the local MacDonalds for everyone. When the tears had stopped and the girls were calmer, they sipped on their coffee while Mr Green took Betty May into his office to find out what had happened.

Joni waited with the other girls but they seemed to be very off hand. Each were trying to think where the watch could have gone. They asked who had come into the office and might have taken it. They knew it wasn't one of them. They wouldn't do such a thing but each were uncomfortable knowing there was a thief in their midst. Joni airily told them it was a lot of fuss over nothing. A watch wasn't anything worth getting so upset over. Shocked at such a heinous thing to say, one of the girls, who seemed to be the ringleader, told Joni in no uncertain terms that it was not just that it was a gorgeous watch and expensive as well but it had been given to her by her boyfriend which made it extra special. She murmured tartly that Joni wouldn't know about that as she hadn't got a boyfriend who would spend that much on her.

Joni dismissed the girl with a shrug of her shoulders and a grimace. It didn't matter to her what they thought.

This had a dramatic effect on the group of girls. They looked at each other, thinking the same thing. The leader again stepped forward and stated in a menacing tone, "It's funny you know, but the thieving only started about the time you came here, Joni Mitchell." She said her name with great contempt. Joni was now angry. She had had this before. Being a new girl, she always got the blame for everything that happened in an office. She was disgusted, angry and humiliated by such an accusation. She told the girls they were vermin to accuse her of such a thing and she hated them. The raised voices brought Mr Green out of his office. Joni by now was crying and told Mr Green what the girls had insinuated. Mr Green took a distraught Joni into his office with Betty May and told the girls to consider an apology to Joni for saying such a dreadful thing. The girls hung their heads and murmured they would.

The day ended badly and Joni went home determined to hand in her notice the next day. She couldn't work with such disgusting, nasty vile people. Only Mr Green was reasonable and nice, the rest were not people she could work with.

So, today she was on her way to London. She was fed up working in small local offices where there were such petty-minded people. She was worth so much more and had great organisational and office skills which would get her a good job. She had booked herself into the YMCA off Tottenham Court Road in London. She was lucky they had a room vacant for her. She had organised an interview tomorrow morning with a nice company in the City and was really looking forward to working with great people who had a more worldly attitude, obviously more in keeping with herself.

Her only concern was the train had been held up for some time now and she was worried she would be late arriving at the YMCA. She wanted to unpack, get something to eat and prepare for her interview tomorrow. A new town, a new company and new people. It was just what she wanted. Anxious now, she rummaged in her bag to find out what the time was. Those watching saw her pull out of her bag a magnificent watch. They saw the watch's rectangular face was nestled in the wristband of links that were rosegold and what looked like alternating bejewelled links. Someone, impressed, raised an eyebrow when they spotted the Swarovski swan on the designer watch face.

THOSE WERE THE DAYS, MY FRIEND

"Oh my gawd, its bloody hot on here," she exclaimed, wiping her brow. Her jacket creaked as she moved her arm.

"Why don't you take your jacket off, dear," the elderly lady ventured. She had watched Sandy fidget and tut for the past hour. The train had been stopped now for a very long time and it was most annoying. Mrs Kelly, she was always called Mrs Kelly, she liked it that way, had thought she had the carriage all to herself. She was going to read her Jane Austin book and enjoy the peace and quiet of the journey when as the train seemed to be pulling out of the station a flurry of hair and leather and cursing pulled open the door and this woman plonked herself down on the seat right opposite Mrs Kelly. She had exhaled with relaxed satisfaction that she had caught the train after all.

She introduced herself. "Hi there, I am Sandy, Sandy Olssen. Looks like we are going to ride pillion together to London." Mrs Kelly looked quizzical and Sandy laughed. "Sorry, that's bike talk. What's your name?"

Mrs Kelly stared for a moment and with an almost belligerent shake of the head, tried to gather together all her dignity and pride and responded, "My name is Mrs Kelly."

Sandy looked at her and was about to say, *OK, but what is your first name,* but she saw the warning glint in Mrs Kelly's eye and decided to be polite. She snuggled down in the seat and with a smile courteously said, "I am pleased to meet you, Mrs Kelly.

With a nod and a near smile, Mrs Kelly returned to her book. She had no wish to talk to this woman who was old enough to know that a black leather jacket with pictures and studs all over it and the metal stud in her nose and lip were just so wrong for what she surmised was a forty-something-year-old woman. She could see she obviously dyed her long hair black from the grey roots that were brazenly apparent across the parting. The skin-tight jeans were quite disgustingly revealing and the boots rather rough for a woman. Sandy caught the look, "Oh, they are my biker boots, Mrs Kelly." Provocatively she looked at Mrs Kelly and added, "Never wear anything else." Again Mrs Kelly nodded, she didn't want to know why she would never wear anything else and returned to her book in the hope that she might at last get some peace and quiet.

Mrs Kelly had recently celebrated her 87th birthday and it had been a two-sherry day. Mrs Kelly only ever had one sherry a day but her birthday had been a very special day. She was on her way to London to see her grandson who lived in America but was in London on business. He was so busy and said he didn't have time to visit her. She had brought up a family of very busy children and the grandchildren had good work ethics too. Her sons Peter and Charles had excellent jobs that took them to Singapore and America. She saw them about once per year but they had families and business commitments. She fully understood this and was very proud of them.

Now the train had stopped for so long the carriage felt hot and stuffy. Sandy got out of her rucksack a bottle of water. "Wanna drop of this, Mrs Kelly?" she asked obligingly. Mrs Kelly just shook her head, the smile still having difficulty appearing. Sandy just grimaced, shrugged her shoulders and took a long drink from the bottle. Mrs Kelly watched this display of bad manners under hooded eyes. The disapproval showed in her face.

They sat in an uncomfortable silence. Mrs Kelly was finding it hard to concentrate on her book. She could feel the woman's eyes intently staring at her and Mrs Kelly kept looking up from her book and acknowledging the interest with a lukewarm smile. Eventually with a loud sigh, Mrs Kelly closed her book sharply, feeling a little embarrassed at the forceful way she had done that. Sandy took this as a good sign. She was bored already and although Mrs Kelly was a stuck-up bitch of a woman, at least they could talk a bit to while away some time. Sandy wasn't used to being patient, she lived life to the full and didn't waste any time. The old lady opposite her had deep lines across her face and every time she looked up at her the lines seemed to have etched even deeper. Mrs Kelly looked like she was just waiting to die. To break the silence Sandy asked, "So, are you fed up with that book, Mrs Kelly? It looked heavy going."

Mrs Kelly wasn't sure how to answer that question. *How do you talk to such a stupid person?* she thought, but mustering up some goodwill she responded nicely, "Well, my dear, it's a classic and such a worthwhile read."

Not convinced and hearing the smarmy one-upmanship in her voice, Sandy crossed her legs and arms and replied with a grunt.

Mrs Kelly came from an old England background and sensing the disquiet in the carriage between them, tried to bring a bit of manners and politeness back into their conversation. With a smile that needed a bit of polishing up, Mrs Kelly cocked her head and summonsing as much interest as she could, asked, "Why are you travelling to London Sandy?"

Sandy now shifted excitedly in her chair. Her legs and arms unfolded now, she leant forward and spilled her thoughts across to a bemused Mrs Kelly.

"Well, this is just so exciting, Mrs Kelly. I just decided to do it. I know I am mad but it happens and you just got to go for it."

Mrs Kelly slightly moved her upper body forward towards Sandy, wondering what she was saying. She was not that interested but Sandy's excitement was catching and she wanted to know more.

"So do tell. What are you going to do?"

Sandy, to be quite honest, wasn't used to anyone interested in what she was doing. She lived by herself in a small flat that had seen better days. She was a cleaner and she worked hard; she had three cleaning jobs. She didn't want to tell Mrs Kelly that. She sensed the stuck-up bitch would look down on her. Cleaning was quite a solitary life but it paid the bills. Going to London was going to change her life. She told herself that but wasn't sure if that was true. If Tony had still been in her life, he would have taken her to London on the back of his motorbike which would have been great but he was long gone. She loved him and they were going to settle down together and tour the country on his bike. They had plans. He would have supported her in this but he left her. She still missed him.

"Well, Mrs Kelly, have you heard of the *X Factor* programme on the television?" Sandy looked unconvinced Mrs Kelly would know what the hell she was talking about.

"Yes, my dear, I have. I watch it every year."

Surprised at this but pleased, Sandy leaned further forward and joyously stated, "Well I am going to be on it. There! What do you think of that?"

Mrs Kelly was a tad surprised by that piece of information and a little concerned. Looking at the Sandy before her, she didn't think she would stand a hope in hell of getting through the audition let alone go on the television.

"What makes you think you will get through the auditions, Sandy. I hear its very hard and there are hundreds of people attending."

"I got a letter inviting me to apply," was the overwhelmingly happy response.

"My goodness," said a shocked Mrs Kelly. "Who sent the letter to you and how have they heard of you?" asked an interested Mrs Kelly, who was getting unusually interested in this conversation.

"Well," said a now subdued Sandy. "My then boyfriend sent a letter and a tape of my singing to the *X Factor*. He sent this a year ago and I got a letter from them last week inviting me to London. How awesome is that?"

"Gosh," said a breathless Mrs Kelly. "So where is your boyfriend. Can't he come with you to see the audition?"

"No, he's gone now so he can't come." Sandy took a deep breath and smiled. "At least I have this opportunity and I am grateful to him for that."

Looking at Sandy, Mrs Kelly assumed she would sing something from that rock-and-roll type music but she had to ask her.

"What will you sing at the *X Factor* when you get to London?"

Sandy smiled.

"You know when I was younger, I so wanted to be a rock star and sing like my idol Axl Rose. He sang 'Sweet Child O'Mine', the best song in the world, singing with AC/DC, the best band in the world." Sandy looked up at Mrs Kelly and sadly added, "I couldn't do it; I just didn't have the right voice to do it."

Mrs Kelly looked at her and thought, *Of course she couldn't sing like Axl Rose, whoever he is, stupid girl and now she was going to go to the* X Factor. *They will tear her apart there.*

"So, what are you going to sing?" asked Mrs Kelly, now wondering what on earth she was going to say. Mrs Kelly knew people who did the karaoke singing things were never that good when they sang alone on the *X Factor*. She had seen enough programmes to know this. They would use this poor girl as the stooge singer they had on every show; the ones that can't sing and everyone laughs at. She was getting worried for this girl now.

Sandy thought the old girl was being rather nice to her and it had been a long time since she had talked about singing.

"Well, Mrs K," she started rather cheekily.

Mrs Kelly wasn't very keen on this abbreviation of her name and it showed in her pout but she didn't want to cause this poor, deluded girl any more trouble than she was walking into going on the *X Factor*.

"It's funny because I can sing, just can't sing rock-and-roll and I would have loved to be a rock-and-roll singer."

She had that faraway look for a moment and then turned to Mrs Kelly and smiled. "But I found the music that suits my voice and I have to tell you, I found this wonderful music that I love too. It's weird and strange and exciting."

Sandy was fully animated now and her cheeks were bright red and her eyes sparkled. Mrs Kelly thought she looked quite beautiful for a second.

"I found opera!"

There was silence for what felt like ages. Sandy looked excitedly into Mrs Kelly's eyes and Mrs Kelly just stared back unable to say or do anything. Sandy broke the silence with, "I will sing 'The Queen of the Night' from *The Magic Flute*, I love that piece, it's one of my favourites."

The silence broken; Mrs Kelly wanted to laugh out loud. That couldn't be right. It's an aria that required a powerful soprano to do that justice. She had to be nice and not laugh at such a preposterous decision.

"That's a powerful aria, my dear," said Mrs Kelly kindly.

"I know but I love it."

Sandy could see that Mrs Kelly wasn't convinced. "I will sing some of it for you if you like."

Mrs Kelly nodded, a little taken aback by such an unlikely offer. What would she say when this Sandy ruins such a beautiful piece? Sandy stood up and composed herself and as she did this suddenly her whole face and body transformed into something quite normal in Mrs Kelly's eyes. Even the awful jacket didn't look quite so bad and the piercings seemed to vanish. Sandy took a deep breath and out of her mouth came the most wonderful soprano voice that Mrs Kelly had ever heard. Sandy managed the whole intricate piece and when finished sat down quietly. Humbled and in awe Mrs Kelly just looked at Sandy. She leant forward and took her hand.

"My dear, that is the most wonderful rendition of the aria I have ever heard. Why have you never been heard before? You are unbelievable."

"Aww thank you, Mrs Kelly, I just listened to records and learned from them. When I was with Tony, I had a few lessons and he was very supportive but when he went, I didn't bother anymore. So, the letter was a nice surprise."

"Where is this Tony. How could he leave such a talented wonderful person?" asked a now-committed fan of Sandy.

"He couldn't help it, Mrs Kelly. He had a motorbike accident about 7 months ago and died."

Sandy suddenly felt overcome. The tears were forming in her eyes but she was a biker gal and crying ain't in her vocabulary and she grimaced and pulled herself together with a determination that the watchful Mrs Kelly found very powerful.

Mrs Kelly, not usually soft-hearted, found tears forming in her eyes which was so unlike her. She wanted to do something and she knew exactly what to do.

"Sandy, I am meeting my grandson in London for

lunch, if this train ever starts again. I want you to come with me and meet him. He will love to meet you."

"Cheers, Mrs Kelly, but I have to get ready for the audition tomorrow and find somewhere to stay as well. There is a YMCA near Tottenham Court Road I need to book into."

Mrs Kelly would have none of it. "You will stay in my hotel at my expense, my dear. My grandson has to meet you today because tomorrow he will be busy sifting through hundreds of auditions. He has been brought over from America to help with the auditions for the *X Factor* and I need him to meet you today."

At that, the train eventually started and the journey to London had taken an unexpected turn for both of them.

POT BLACK

A Study of Life

"Can you ring the signal box again?" asked Peter, a very fed-up young man. Old Tom as he was called was the train driver and Peter was his second man or fireman as his position would have been called. The driver's compartment was full of dials and equipment to run the electric train but at present it was all at a standstill. They had finished the flasks of coffee and sandwiches they had brought for the journey to London and should have been arriving at the terminal by now. They had been at a standstill for over an hour and the usually comfortable driver's compartment was feeling hot and claustrophobic and they both stared at the red traffic light outside willing it to turn green.

Old Tom was 56 years old and looked older than his age with heavy creases that hung from his face. His nose and cheeks looked like they had imbibed many glasses of something alcoholic and his eyes were permanently slitted in a quizzical look. He had been asked this same question for the last hour and he was fed up with it. He yanked his glasses of his nose in a fit of annoyance. He looked at this streak of piss with red hair and a moustache that looked more like bum fluff than hair and with a sigh replied, "We will get a message when the train is ready to start and that red light," and he jabbed a finger at the traffic lights, "will turn green!" He almost shouted the last bit. This was something that seemed to happen far too regularly on this line but they were being paid so a little patience was called for.

Peter, aggrieved by Old Tom's attitude, blushed; something he did quite often and it embarrassed him, and shook his head from side to side as he tried to justify his question.

"Well, it's just that I am expected at our social club canteen tonight for a tournament. I am doing well and I have worked hard for this. The table is calling me and I reckon to pot the black tonight."

Old Tom lightened up. "You play snooker? Well, I haven't been there for a while now since I hurt my back. I can't bend over the table like I used to and if I can't play properly, I would rather not play."

Peter grunted at this unwanted bit of information.

"Yeh," said Old Tom, as he raised himself up to his full height and looked at this kid with distain. "I used to be the reigning champion."

Peter didn't believe this old man. He grimaced and said, "I thought that was Thomas Lyons who was the champion? I am gonna beat his record of 7 years as the snooker champion of the RMT." (National Union of Rail, Maritime and Transport Workers.) "That's one hell of a record to beat and no one has done it yet, but I reckon I can," said a very ambitious Peter. Old Tom looked at him and smirked.

"I am Thomas Lyons and you have got to work hard to beat my record, you bastard!!"

Peter ignored the insult and in awe, breathed. "You are he?"

Pleased at such adoration, Old Tom replied smugly, "Yup!"

"Well," said a now very excited Peter, "I am playing ASLEF members tonight. I beat the top player in a competition at RMT, Stephen Goodly, do you know him?"

"Nah," said Old Tom. "To be honest I don't follow it much now. When I couldn't play anymore, I went off the game."

Peter didn't understand that. How could anyone go off such a magnificent game, especially after being the heroic 7-year champion. It shocked him and he wondered if Old Tom was just old now and perhaps, he shouldn't even be driving trains.

In the silence Old Tom was thinking and after a minute or so he asked, "So how long have you been playing?"

"Well." Peter smacked his lips as he recalled the years. "I have been playing since I was 16 years old."

Old Tom didn't think Peter looked much older than 16 years now. He asked Peter, "So how old are you now?"

"Ooh, I'm 20 years old now, so I've been playing a long while."

"So how often do you practise?" asked Old Tom.

"I practise 3 times a week." Peter smiled and grunted "My woman isn't keen on that I can tell you."

"You've got a woman at your age?" asked Old Tom. "You married already?"

"Nah, not married, we just live together." He saw the look of dismay on Old Tom's face and added quickly, "We will get married later, when we have saved some money. The kid takes all our money at the moment."

"You have a kid?"

Peter felt under attack and tried to explain. "Well, you see, it sort of happened and we had Peter Junior. We rented a flat and are waiting to save up enough to buy a house one day. I can make a bit of money betting on the games so that's what I am doing."

"Is she a good woman?" asked Old Tom. Peter thought that a very strange question. "Yeh, she is great and I want to marry her eventually and she wants to marry me." He blurted out, "We love each other," and then felt embarrassed for saying such a thing to this man. To sound more macho, Peter added, "She will back me up while I practise and try and get more money so we can get married and get a home. This job, with its shift work and extra hours is pretty tough on her with the baby but we will get there."

Old Tom nodded at this and quite liked this lad. This was the first time they had worked together and he thought he was just another bastard looking to earn some money as easily as possible and then going off to drink it all away. He hadn't got much time for the youngsters today. His own 2 sons were a waste of space and they had coloured his view of all young men. Old Tom was known as a misery by most other drivers. This one was worth helping and Old Tom decided to give him his wise thoughts on how he became an unbeaten 7-year Snooker Champion of the RMT. He knew they had at least another half an hour before the red stop light would turn to green. His experience had been that this stop time would go on for another half an hour. Enough time to put this lad straight.

Old Tom rubbed his hands together, took a deep breath and asked Peter, "Would you like some advice on how to become a 7-year snooker champion?"

Peter, wide-eyed and grateful said, "Yes please. To get advice from the master is wonderful, thank you."

Old Tom nearly smiled at that. This was a very pleasant conversation and it didn't happen often to him these days. I am not sure if Old Tom realised it himself but most people avoided him these days. He used to be fun and there used to be banter with him but over the last two years he had become a miserable, moaning old man and most thought life was too short to listen to his rubbish so he was avoided like the plague.

Old Tom smacked his lips together as he thought how to start and then with a deep breath he began. "So the most important part of snooker is practice. I don't mean a bit of practice; I mean lots and lots of practice." He could see Peter opening his mouth to say something but he raised his hand so he could finish.

"No ifs or buts, it paramount that you practise every day. Now me." And Old Tom pointed to himself and with high pride informed Peter of his ritual for practising. "I got up at 6a.m. and went straight to the canteen and I practised until 8a.m. then I had breakfast and depending on my rota, I would either go to work or stay until my rota started."

Peter had to interrupt at this time. "But what if your rota had a 6p.m. start? Did you go home?"

With pride Old Tom said, "No, I would stay until

6p.m. You can never practice enough. If I was on an early rota I would stay until at least 8p.m. practising and then go home to bed so I could get up early for the early rota." He looked at Peter with a puffed-out chest. "I was proud of my commitment to snooker and my ability to continue being the snooker champion for 7 years."

Peter asked, "But what about your dinner, your meals. When did you have them?"

Old Tom looked at him with distain and mockingly said, "Where do you think I ate? At our canteen, of course. That's what it is there for." Old Tom laughed at this naïve comment, it was obvious, wasn't it?

Peter digested these comments and asked, "So, for how long did you practise all those many hours per day?"

Old Tom thought for a moment. It was obvious to him what the answer was, but the lightweight lad here just wasn't getting it. "I did it for 7 years, you stupid bastard. Do you think you can just stop trying to get better? I have gotta tell you the competition gets stronger every year. There is always someone on your back waiting to take your championship away." Old Tom thought for a moment, he wanted to make it a bit clearer for this thick and stupid lad who just wasn't seeing the bigger picture. "It's like being a champion gunslinger."

Peter raised his eyebrows at this comment. Old Tom, now into it, continued, "There is always someone wanting to bring you down so you have to practise, practise, practise and I did."

Peter, surprised and a little unsure, asked, "What did your wife think of you being out so much?"

"Oh well." And Old Tom stopped, he had to think about that. "I think she was OK. To be honest, I didn't see her very much." He was quiet for a moment and then with great pride added, "I brought home the money and she never went without. I was a good provider."

Peter wanted to ask more but thought it a bit indelicate to enquire if he missed his wife or she missed him. He wondered if they had time for a romantic night together during those 7 years. The question was going to be answered in part as Old Tom, deep in thought continued.

"I was red-hot in all my competitions." He added with immense pride "I had been told I could go professional but well, I loved my job so didn't consider it."

Peter nodded courteously and smiled. This was one hell of a committed man to his job and his snooker. He felt inferior to this giant of a man. Silently he watched Old Tom who was still deep in thought.

"What I did, Peter, when a big competition came up, was special. I have to tell you when you are really good, these competitions come thick and fast and you have to be ready. What I did was I slept in the canteen back room where they had settees so I didn't waste time travelling to practise snooker. For quite a few years, at the height of my fame, I slept many nights at the canteen so I could work and practise. I would go home for clean washing and to say hello. I sacrificed a lot to be a 7-year champion. You have to be prepared to walk the walk if you want to do that."

Just as he finished his sentence, the radio crackled and some disembodied voice told Old Tom that the light was about to change to green. Opening up the intercom, Old Tom informed the passengers that they were about to move and would be in London in approximately one hour.

As they moved on their way and the train reached a comfortable speed, Peter asked Old Tom what he would do when he got to the station.

"I am going straight home. Get something to eat and watch a film. I am quite a homebody these days."

Peter said, "I bet your wife is glad to hear that after your epic time as a snooker champion."

Old Tom looked at Peter and with a slight tinge of something, Peter wondered if it was sadness or regret or something like that Old Tom said, "Nah. She left me 2 years ago. I never knew why, she wouldn't say." Peter watched while Old Tom sat looking into space for a moment and then his demeanour changed into an angry stance. "She was a selfish cow, I worked hard for her and she just sodded off with the boys. She remarried last year to some tosspot. I reckon she was having an affair whilst I was working hard. The bitch!"

The journey went fast enough and when they arrived at the terminal, both Peter and Old Tom picked up their bags and bits and pieces and made their way to their lockers in the canteen. They put away anything they wanted to store there and turned to leave.

Old Tom turned to Peter and asked, "Was my talk helpful to you?"

Peter smiled. "It was ace, Tom. I would have made a big mistake if I hadn't spoken to you. Thank you very much indeed. I will always remember your words."

Old Tom smiled. Glad he could help the young man. He walked slowly towards the train that would take him home to his cold empty house. He hated walking into the house when it was dark and cold. With a deep breath he picked up his feet, straightened his back and just remembered he was the snooker champion for 7 whole years. He didn't think that young man would make the grade and challenge his record. *Young men are not made of sterner stuff these days*, he thought, *they are a load of wimps.*

Peter, when he got outside the station, rang home on his mobile. He told his girlfriend about the delay on the train and that he was coming home. She asked about his game tonight and he said he wasn't going to it. He asked if she had eaten yet and she hadn't. He said he was bringing home a takeaway and a bottle of something so they could have a romantic evening together to celebrate. She asked him what were they celebrating and he told her he was celebrating having her in his life and their son. He learned a big lesson tonight and it had nothing to do with snooker.

This book is printed on paper from sustainable sources managed under the Forest Stewardship Council (FSC) scheme.

It has been printed in the UK to reduce transportation miles and their impact upon the environment.

For every new title that Troubador publishes, we plant a tree to offset CO_2, partnering with the More Trees scheme.

MORE TREES
LET'S PLANT A BILLION TREES

For more about how Troubador offsets its environmental impact, see www.troubador.co.uk/sustainability-and-community